D1571928

Rockspring

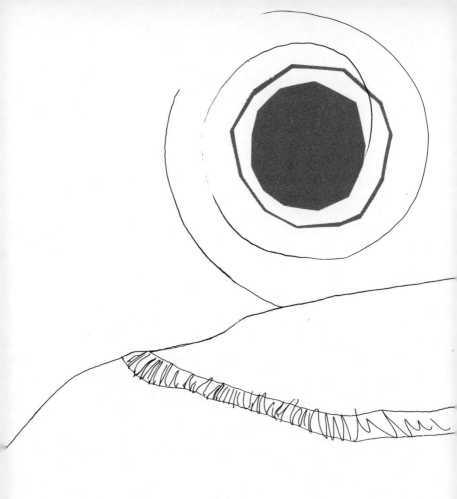

Rockspring

R. G. VLIET

THE VIKING PRESS   NEW YORK

For Ann

These delicates he heap'd with glowing hand
On golden dishes and in baskets bright
Of wreathed silver: sumptuous they stand
In the retired quiet of the night
　　　　　　—KEATS, *The Eve of St. Agnes*

Rockspring

ONE

exas, 1830, and they were barefoot and hadn't ought to be, for they'd roused up a rattler already this morning to crawling on its bellyscales. But she allowed it was the sun brought it out, for all it was October. And it was a fine sun, to reach down between the trees and piece the ground to such a yellow and darkness at her feet.

Jensie walked through the leaves, it felt so good. Thousands and thousands of leaves, as if fall like some painted Indian had shot them down—pecan leaves, all yellow and spotted and pointing to a sharpness that half tickled her feet, and curled up and nicked her ankles as she crunched them. Now if every arrowhead the Indians ever shot was to be raked together, she thought, would they at all fill the whole ground like this, I wonder? This one patch of trees near the river.

Here was a sunny place. Jensie stooped down. She set her gourd careful on the ground and commenced picking fat leaves of sheepsorrel from their straws. These grow like arrowheads too. But they can't hurt you. Jensie rubbed her forefinger across a leaf's soft undersides. Mix them with vinegar for rhubarb pie. Mama'll be proud to get them. Jensie stuffed the leaves into the gourd. Now she almost had a gourdful.

"Jensie," her little brother cried up in a fret, "the Injuns'll *git* you if you don't quit pickin' their veggables." Then, with all the orneriness he had in him, he eased a stem between two of his toes and hiked it up, scattering dirt from its roots everywhere.

"Quit it, Dee, can't you?" Jensie said. "Don't you want Mama to make us no rhubarb pie?"

"I wanna go home. It's dinner. Them leafs is too old anyways, and Mama'll toss 'em right back out. Come on, Jensie, you got us all the way downstream. We can't even hear Daddy choppin'." Their daddy in the brush-clearing near the cabin, chopping cornstalks to winter-feed the cow. And it was Jensie's birthday almost—just two more weeks—and that's when they would have their first bread since they come here. A party. Mama was saving the first time for that. Grated corn skillet-bread mixed with milk, and yes her a new dress made from that chambry in the chest, brought all the way from San Antonio, and yes she was fourteen might'near and for sure wasn't going to let Dee boss her.

"Well, I want a great big juicy green rhubarb pie for supper," Jensie said.

4

"We got us a whole sackful of pee-cans up under that tree there," Dee said. "That's what we was sent for. Not no stinkin' veggables."

Because he was such a bother sometimes, no good at all, and sometimes she just hated him; and sometimes she reckoned she loved him—when he was littler mostly and couldn't all the time bother her. She used to hold him wrapped in a piece of blanket back in Mississippi, and sit on a scrubbed bench in the sun, and sing to him Sandy Land.

Jensie hummed Sandy Land and went right on picking. Because Dee wasn't going to bother her, no sirree.

Dee sat plop onto the gound. "Jackass," he said, and that was enough for a fight, the little brat, but she wasn't going to let him rile her, and she went right on picking. And when they got home, Mama would hear about *that*. Dee begun spinning around and around on his back like a top or a turtle, scattering leaves everywhere.

Jensie rose.

"Are you comin'?" she said.

"No no no no," Dee said. "I'm tired of follerin' after you."

"All right. Stay there then and let the Indians git you," Jensie said. "Burn a coal to your nose." She begun to walk toward the river. In a minute, Dee got up and knocked the leaves from his britches and hung along after. Well, she was sorry she'd scared him with Indians, but he ought not to have crossed her.

But pretty soon, when they were back under the trees, Dee was right along with. Now the sunlight fell down onto them again like so many warmish feathers stripped from their shafts by the high, knifing pecan branches. That woman once, just this side of San Antonio, who'd come out from hiding in the woods and seen her loved ones scalped. Happened just before her and Daddy and Mama and Dee drove up. There that woman was, walking around about her yard. Benches and broken dishes. And everywhere, all hung on fences and bushes, was feathers that the Indians had shook from the ticks—the Indians had only wanted the ticks. And this woman not paying no mind at all to her and Daddy and Mama and the rest, but just stumbling around about her yard, trying to pick back her blown bed-feathers. Jensie shivered. She was about to think her ownself a scare. Well, she wasn't going to let *Dee* know it, and then talk her into running home like a fool.

Yes, it had got powerful hot, and she was going to take her own sweet time, and maybe even have her a swim. And then go home.

Thank God they hadn't seen an Indian since they come here.

The sound of the river was cool and the sun full bright onto it. Jensie pushed her way through some redbud and hackberry.

"Now where're you goin'?" Dee said.

"I figured to maybe take me a swim," Jensie said. She almost laughed then. Dee's face had rounded up into a little red fist. He let out a noise from his gullet as if he'd gagged on a cricket. Then he flung himself down, all the time making that cricket noise, and started butting his head onto the ground and kicking around in the hackberry thicket like he was going to dig himself a hole, he was such a baby.

"There's some purty rocks here you can git," Jensie said. "Or you can build yourself some twig-houses and go visitin'," she said. "I'll only be a minute." Dee rolled over onto his back. His eyes were big as a pair of yellow plums. He snapped his head at her like he'd like to bite her. "Whump whump whump," he said. It was awful funny.

Jensie didn't laugh, though. She wasn't going to be mean to him. And now where she stood the sun bore down onto her. The hackberries and redbuds weren't much shade. The sun pressed her back and her neck. It made her hair feel close and sticky. The back of her dress was so dry and cottony, it was about to burn up. And maybe she hadn't really thought to go swimming—it was just to tease this little sissy—but now she made up her mind she'd do it. She didn't know when she'd get another chance. There was chores to do when they got home, inside that stuffy cabin; and then pretty soon it was going to be winter, and she wouldn't get another chance this year at all.

"You stay right here," Jensie said. "I'm only goin' out on that bar there, where that broomwiller is, and don't you look." On account of Dee couldn't go with her. That wouldn't be right. And he didn't like to swim anyway.

"Well, I reckon I seen enough," Dee said, wiping dirt and snot from his nose. "I seen you undressin' a-plenty of times, nights, in the cabin."

Jensie's face turned red. "You better not have!" she said. "You was supposed to be sleepin'."

Dee said, "Weren't nothin' to see no-ways."

Jensie nearly hit him then. She well-nigh did. But instead, she tucked her gourd tight under her arm and turned and pushed out through the bushes and onto the riverbed. People in India walk on stones hot as these. But in a minute Jensie stepped into the water, and it was cool and slippery to her feet. The water swished over her feet. The stones beneath were soft and rounded; their cold reach shot up through her shinbones to a sweet ache, and it was so cool it was like saying a prayer that kept her feet safe as she stepped out onto the rocks of the gravel bar—little round hot puddings of quartz and mealy granite—and walked across them to the broomwillow.

Jensie rested a mite beneath the willow, which wasn't much more than a three-limbed thing leaning downstream from a power of old floods. The sun peeled back the wet from Jensie's ankles. Jensie looked at the river. This here was the Nueces, and a prettier river she never did see. Not that old Sabine river they'd crossed to Texas over. *That* one was worse than a bayou, water thicker than week-old coffee, and the high tangle-rooted mudbanks, and away off on both sides, the salt-grass marsh. Nor the Trinity, nor the Brazos. Nor the Colorado, neither. The Colorado had reminded Jensie of nothing so much as an old fat-backed water moccasin winding down-country. They'd crossed all those rivers, yes, and more, but this here was the prettiest river she ever did see. It was open to the sun, clear and trickle-tongued, didn't need to keep no secrets. It was that clear, you could have seen your heart through it. Why, Jensie could see the bottom right from where she sat. And along on both sides, it

8

was a white road, each stone of it scrubbed cleaner than a drinking-gourd by the water and the sun. Road for a king. This here river. Down from the canyon country and far lonesome places. Hemmed and spangled with green. The trees on both sides—mostly pecans, but some live oaks, red oaks, elms—grew way up tall, they were that proud to be here. And the hackberries and redbuds and broomwillows and box elders grew small, near the river, they were that humble. It was a fearful-strong and gentle king, this here river. Just look on this broomwillow she was sitting under. It leans, but still comes green. And all the green things around about were a fresh bright green, from the hand that fed them. Think of fish: bass and bullheads and drum: what lives this river leads! And nothing better for a body to drink. Cold, sweet, clean as the insides of a stone down your gullet.

Or for to swim in.

Jensie set the gourd against the roots of the willow and hummed Sandy Land. She undid the pin at the knob of her neck and pulled off her dress, over her head. Now she stood in her shift. She hung the dress onto the willow. That old ugly thing, how she'd be glad to be rid of it. It'd been three times dyed in indigo and piss, and was tore under the left armpit, and was a tatter to see. How she craved for that new chambry! She could hardly wait. Because *then* look at her.

She took out her tucking comb. Her hair fell down about her shoulders. She had the prettiest hair. That's why she needed that new dress: to set off that hair. She never seen no other like it. It was pure white. Her mama didn't have hair like that, nor her daddy neither. *His* hair was yellow. But plenty of folks had

9

hair her daddy's color. Jensie'd never seen nobody else, though, that had hair like hers. Everybody always remarked on Jensie's hair, whenever first they seen her. It was so soft and white and shiny, the color of winter stubble or a junco's breast-feathers.

That hot sun.

Now Jensie stepped into the water. Oh it was delicious. It drenched the hem of her shift. Now she let herself down into it—oh it was cold! It was colder than she'd figured, and Jensie let out a squeal. Then it felt better. Jensie turned over in the water. She grabbed hold of the stones on the bottom and kicked and splashed in the water, the kind of harshness that gave way beneath her legs. It was so crisp-cold it numbed the undersides of her arms. It scrubbed away her goosebumps. She let her hair that was the color of water stream downstream. The water lifted her body, tried to coax her downstream. Oh this here river never said a word. It just tickled her ears, made a popping hurt in her head. It twisted and tugged her shift loose about her. It was even a mite pert. When Jensie sat up, facing downstream, it gave a shove to her hips; then the bottom scrambled out from under her and for a minute she was kicking and laughing and lost. But somehow she got back onto her feet.

She stood up. The river in a great drench from off her, and her shift tight as a skin onto her and hurting the nubbins of her breasts. Dee had better not be looking.

The only trouble with this here river, Jensie thought, is that you can see *through* it, but never catch your *wholeself* in it, it's so all the time moving. Like that splinter of a mirror back in the cabin. What was left of a whole one. You could see your eyes, maybe, could see the color of your hair, could grin at it for your teeth's sake, but never see the *all* of you at once, so that you never knew really who you were.

Drippings speckled the stream; and wet trickles down her face, tangles of wet hair to her neck. Jensie tossed her head. The sun swept her face. Her hair flew in threads of bright. That was when she seen the three Mexicans.

She didn't waste no time, but started running through the water. DEE! That river—was slow—as ropes at her thighs. The horse was at her. Jensie turned and fell in the water. She seen the horse's hoofs—their undersides—and wide nostrils, eyes, a flail of white wet belly as the horse nearly trampled her. Mexican was off saddle into water with a bust of splash, had a grab of her tight against his belly. God what a screech then she let up. But it was half a passel of choke-bubbles, because she was down under the water, chunked down under: wild squirrelly thing for kicks, bone-crackings, sights breaking through her eyes. A flush of stonesuck jugged her chest. Sudden somewhere a high wind creaked. Then her whole flesh snapped.

Jensie was looking at the ground. The ground was moving underneath her. It was the stones of the river-bed. Her hands, flapping loose as broken birdwings, nearly touched them. She was flung across the withers of a horse. She could see the horse's hoofs onto the stones. And her belly felt broken half in two, and her innards pushed nearly into her gullet. She was about to choke; her head was upside-down, heavy-blooded. Water was gagging in her mouth.

Jensie moaned. Suddenly she felt a *slap!* and the sting of it on her bottom. It made her suck in breath.

Men laughed, whoever they were. And that man sitting in the saddle above her—his big knees pressing against her legs and back, binding her—laughed. The horse stopped walking. The man got off the horse and dragged Jensie down onto the riverbed. Jensie lay there a minute. She wondered was she dead, the sky was so white. Then she seen them. Those Mexicans' faces spun around and around above her—sometimes two, sometimes three faces of a kind, and seven grins, and sixteen sets of eyes. Until Jensie pulled herself together. Then her eyes come clear. She seen then that there were just three faces. Three mean ones. A fat, thick, hog-jowled one, the color of a coffeebean, dark as Egypt, yellow-and-red-eyed, filled with grin under a greasy handlebar. And a young one, mean-Mexican-eyed. Then Jensie seen that the third man was an Indian, and that put a worse scare in her. His face was high-cheeked, dry shiny acorn color, and his nostrils wide. He had a scar beneath his left eye. It cut dark and thick-mended across his cheek. But it was his eyes mostly that scared her: straight thread-thin upper lids that gave a slit to his eyes as he watched her—eyes black as night or whatever all it was he was figuring behind them to do to her. Jensie cried out *Daddy!* and tried to crawl away. But one of the men caught hold of her leg. Then the fat one sat on top of her, laughing like thunder. He pressed a hand to her nose and mouth. It was a taste of smoke and horse. Jensie squeaked like a rabbit, and then couldn't breathe. And when, in a minute, he got up, Jensie just lay there on the stones, sick to her stomach, crying sort of soft-like.

O how Jensie prayed inside herself that her daddy'd come! She craved to see the face of him. Cried, thinking on him and little Dee and poor Mama. Now a hundred times she thought she heard their voices, calling to her. But it was all inside her head—what she *wished* she heard. Pretty soon it died down to an ache and a whisper. She was alone. Nothing, nothing, nothing between her and whatever.

The two Mexicans talked. Jensie reckoned it was Spanish that come out of those Mexicans' mouths. Queer, slippery noises. It might have been so many stones or sticks rubbed together, for all she could make of it. But she didn't care. She just lay there, shaking in her shift.

The fat Mexican leaned over Jensie and brushed a finger against her cheek. Smoke. Horse smell. He wore a crucifix hanging by a leather thong from his neck. The crucifix criss-crossed Jensie's eyes. The Mexican pulled Jensie's hair. "Güera. Una grulla blanca," he said. This fetched a laugh from the others. The Mexican put a thumb against Jensie's neck. Jensie didn't move a whit. The Mexican chuckled. Then he said something in Spanish. It must have meant "Get up," because when Jensie didn't do it, the Mexican hoisted her by the armpits and shoved her toward the horse. It was a coyote-colored horse, what they call a Spanish stick: one of those scraggly, black-maned, long-whiskered kind of horses. The horse gave a start when Jensie bumped against him. He turned his head to see her. He hadn't but one good and one glass eye. There was such a milky emptiness in that one glass eye.

The coyote horse had a stripe down his back, and another that crossed it at the withers. The fat Mexican touched where the two stripes crossed and then crossed himself and laughed. Jensie couldn't make out what it was he said. But she didn't care. She just leaned against the horse and let her hair hang down and all the sun burn down onto her. Then the fat Mexican hoisted her up onto the coyote's withers. There wasn't anything she could do to stop it.

The Mexican boy and the Indian had a Spanish mule and they climbed onto it. The fat Mexican climbed up behind Jensie. He clicked his tongue. The two animals started up the river.

Fast. Faster than Jensie had reckoned these sticks could make it. *Oh Daddy, come save me!* And she thought she heard Dee call her; she tried to slide from the horse. But the Mexican jerked her hair. He said a word in Spanish. For a long while he didn't let loose of her hair; each time he jerked it, it set her eyes to tears. But finally he had to let go: the horse was stumbling in the river. The Mexican pulled at the reins to head it up. That river had got fierce, had begun to take on new ways. It was way upstream now, Jensie could tell that. The river was thinner and crookeder and meaner. It had gone Indian. It had the talk of a wild thing—feathers of spray, hatchet-flashes of reflected light. It cut a wound into the banks, the start of canyons; it sucked pitholes on the downward side of rocks. Only stern, lonely critters could stand to live here: a hookjawed bass. And the brush hung over as if to hide the river's narrowing savagery. Jensie prayed

that they would stick to this river and the horses
would leave droppings on the rocks and it not come
down a rain, so that her daddy could track her.

The horses rested, standing in the water. The
Mexicans let them drink. The Indian slid from the
mule and pulled off two big double-headed gourds and
begun to fill them with water. Jensie was so grieved,
she wished she could be sprinkled to nothing on that
water. She couldn't think straight nor crooked nor any
way except to crave for her mama and Dee and her
daddy daddy daddy! away downstream. The fat Mexican touched her leg—it cut the breath right out of her.
He grinned. "Toral," he said, pointing to himself,
scraping his fingernail against the crucifix. "El Escorpión." He poked his thumb into her leg. Jensie jerked
away from it and he laughed. She threw herself
against the horse's neck and dug her face into its
mane. Her thoughts were dark as that mane.

The Indian flung the gourds across the mule and
climbed on up. *Don't leave this river!* But the fat
Mexican jabbed his heel into the coyote's belly. The
horse didn't want to do it—branches swatted its nose
and chest—but the Mexican forced it up through the
brush.

The horse plundered up an embankment and into
an open space.

They didn't stop but a minute. But it was time
enough. Jensie could see the whole country. It carved
a worse grief in her. The river below, roped by thickets
between two slopes, wound way down, and then broke
free with a shout of light into the open valley, and
then was caught up again between trees. Where she'd

swum, where she'd picked pecans, where she'd eaten and worked and spoke a known tongue. That whole valley was a funnel narrowing, forcing her up to this.

The sun poured its last orange settlings into the valley; the west sides of the live oaks on the riverline down there burned bright as embers. But the trees on the other side of the river were darksome, faraway— that lonesome feeling of evening and goodbye.

Of a sudden Jensie cried out in English *to be let free!* and jumped from the horse. The Mexicans shouted. The fat one spurred his horse to catch her. But Jensie didn't run—she knew that wasn't any use. She only grabbed the fat Mexican's knee and begged to be let free. She cried. She said in English her daddy would pay them anything they wanted. Anything. She swore she wouldn't let on to her daddy a word about them. She swore it. She'd walk back home her ownself and never open her mouth. She swore it.

The Mexican looked down at her, his greasy jacket full of belly, his eyes red-and-yellow beneath his beargrass hat. The crucifix dangled. He said words to her in Spanish. The other two laughed. Then he pulled her back up onto the horse. O never never see her people more! Never hear a sound of English! Lost! Gone barren as those canyon places she was headed for. The colorless country. Dry-grass hills, and clumps of brush. Where nothing is except deer to make a clatter on the rocks, bear to push their fur through cedar, the pad of soft-foot cats. And Indians and wolves and rattlers, and desperate men.

Here on the ridge the wind blew. Jensie shook all through herself from it; her whole flesh fretted on her bones. The wind pushed big sobs out of her. The Mexican wrapped a blanket around her. It stunk of his sweat, and of dust and smoke and guns and horse lather. It made her shake the more. Then the horse and mule turned and climbed up toward the canyons.

About dark they come to a canyon. The Indian stoned a mulerabbit at the mouth of it. It was sure a surprise to that rabbit. Then they started up the canyon. They went a long way up the canyon, it getting all the time darker and colder, October, and the canyon walls closer. Nothing but rocks—little rocks, fair-to-middling rocks, big slabs of boulders. And here and there, clutches of laurel and scrub cedar. It was a dry canyon. There wasn't a lick of water. The horse and mule must have had eyes for dark, and deer bones in their hocks, because they picked their way easy between the rocks. Never a clatter nor slip—just the regular click of hoofs, creak of crosstrees, slosh in the gourds of water. At last they come to an open space.

It was way past dark. The Mexicans hobbled the mule and the horse. The Mexican boy took the crosstrees off the glass-eyed coyote. The coyote let out a long screech of grief when he did it. Its back was raw and bleeding from the crosstrees. The horse rolled on the ground, twisting and scrubbing its wounds against the rocks. Its cries from the dark of horse-grief, and the upheaval and thump of horseflesh, were awful to hear. Jensie feared the horse had gone loco. But the Mexicans never paid no mind to it. They set about skinning the rabbit and building a fire. After a spell, the horse got back onto his feet. Jensie heard him shaking his flanks and withers. Then he moved close to the mule and begun to snuff in the dark for grass.

The three men hunched next to the fire. Though they didn't have their eyes on Jensie, she could tell that they knew every minute what she was doing. She crouched under a scrub cedar, with that stinking blanket wrapped around her, and it cold now, and it night, and October. She watched the three men. They must have been murderers, she thought. Folks must have looked up from their sleep at them, surprised for a minute behind their dying eyes. Those Mexicans must have cut throats, got blood under their thumbnails, took rings from dead women's fingers—even that boy has got fingers long for to choke with. And that Indian—how many scalps had he took? Black hair, brown hair, yellow hair, tow hair.

The Indian leaned over the fire and set the rabbit onto the coals. Jensie could hear the rabbit cramp and sizzle. The Indian was nearly naked, and his legs glistened coppery in the light. Just about all he had on was a blanket that come to his hips, with a hole in the top for his head to poke through. And those two Mexicans weren't dressed in much else either. They each wore wide-brimmed beargrass hats with oily, pointed crowns. The fat Mexican wore a bloody, dark, greasy jacket, open, showing his chest and belly. The Mexican boy had a pair of dirty white belts crossing his chest, but he didn't have a shirt either. Just those two dirty white belts. The fat one was the only one who wore boots. The other two were barefoot. Both of the Mexicans had on blue britches with red stripes down

18

the sides. Jensie reckoned those two Mexicans must have been soldiers once, sent to stir up trouble in Texas. They had plenty of knives and such in their belts to prove it.

The Indian grabbed up the rabbit and tossed it to the fat Mexican, who bit off strips of meat from its half-cooked side and made smacking noises as he chewed them. He handed the carcass to the boy. The boy bit off a chunk and then gave the rabbit back to the Indian. The Indian set the rabbit down on its other side onto the coals; and it hadn't laid there hardly long enough to get warm when he fetched it up and bit into the half-raw flesh. Then he broke the rabbit and passed it three ways. They didn't give Jensie a speck.

After they'd eaten, they passed around a big book that the Indian had kept hung by a thong to the saddle crosstrees, among his gourds. They tore out pages. The Indian passed around some stalks of weed that he'd picked. The Mexicans stripped narrow white leaves from the stalks and rolled the leaves in pages and lit them for a smoke.

Owls hooted from one side of the canyon to the other. Things stirred in the brush. It was an October night and the stars were down close. They were awful cold stars. It hurt Jensie's eyes to look at them. She was lost as those stars, and she knew it. And the cold dried her eyes so. She had to close her eyes to shut out those cold stars. She pulled the blanket tight about her, but still the cold come through, and cedar needles pricked her skin.

The mule and the horse shifted in the dark.

Jensie wished she was home, in her cedar-picket

cabin. She wished she was in her one-legged bed, between the shucks and quilt, and watching a thousand-legger on the rafter. Would he fall onto her bed? Those things have got a poison crawl and leave a red track. The greasewick lamplight lit the cabin. But first she was out in the clearing. Her daddy was plowing along behind Ginger, with his wooden mold-board and homemade stocks, turning up the rich, dark bottomland. And her and Dee following after, picking up stones. They had a whole pile full in the southwest corner of the clearing, those they could lift. Enough almost to start a fence with. But it was darker and there was a mourning dove sounding in the corner. They washed their hands and faces, and Mama dried them on her apron before she let them in the door. They put down *thunk* the oaken drawbar and pulled in the latchstring. The little greasewick was sputtering in the gourd, and gave a light to the whole cabin. What wind was that? It was blowing that wick. It come through an open chink in the cabin. It blew onto her face. Jensie pulled her quilt up tight over her. Something was scratching, breathing at that chink.

Jensie's eyes popped open. It was the fat Mexican above her, breathing onto her. His face was dark as night, and the long black hair. Jensie let out a screech that come to nothing in his fist. She twisted; she pushed against the press of him. Toral's mustache dragged, black wing dragging across her face. The cold, silver crucifix stung her throat. A redwinged blackbird courting once. Toral's tongue clicked in his fat cheeks for all the way of a redwinged blackbird. His yellow-red eyes: spots on stiff wings. And the cluck of the bird, the squatty flutter, and then God how he sprung—beak clacking in her lips, fierce chirrups to her neck, needle-toed bird-grips at her breasts. She flung herself sideways. But he pushed her, spread her wide: a give of bird bone, a parting of feathers.

TWO

All Jensie craved for was to die. She ached with a grief through every bone of her. She had craved all night for death to come. Two dark men had come to her, biting her neck like foxes. Only the boy had not come; there had been laughter. And death had not come. Jensie had begged the two men, cried for them to cut her throat for her, and let her grief free. They only cut her with softer knives. Now the sun rose.

Up above the canyon the sky was tall and pale. Down here it was dark—rock and brush shadows. The Mexican boy and the Indian moved like shadows among the rocks and caught the two horses and un-hobbled them, and tied on their hackamores.

22

Toral walked over to Jensie. He leaned above her. He held out a handful of dry corn. She hated him. She shut her eyes against him. "Grullita blanca," Toral said. "¿Ahora sí comes, eh?"

Jensie couldn't make out a word of it. And she didn't care. She hated him. She turned her face to the cedar needles. She grabbed a tight hold to the cedar bush. She wasn't ever going to eat. She wasn't ever going anywhere. She was going to hang onto this bush, and stay here, and die here. Those Mexicans would have to cut off her hands first, if they aimed to fetch her any farther.

Toral laughed. "¡Bernardino, pronto!" he shouted. "¡Traeme la mula!" "Ah, mi Grullita," he said to Jensie. He put a very sad sound to it. He touched her hair. "Mi corazón. ¿Conoces la agarita, el granjeno?"

Bernardino fetched the mule. The mule was full of a morning orneriness, but he followed Bernardino. There was a horsehair rope coiled to the mule's tail. Toral took one end of it and tied it to Jensie's wrist so tight it cut the blood off. Toral leaned down to Jensie until his mustache touched her cheek. She dug her face into the needles. "Ay, Grullita, Grullita," he said, "no seas tan terca." Then he said, "¡Aha! ¿Conque la grullita quiere tirar raíces con el pico, eh?"

He climbed up onto the mule.

Jensie felt the first tug. She grabbed to the cedar bush with all her might. She bit her teeth so tight it brought tears to her eyes. The mule took a step. O God, how she wished she was one of those roots, dug way down, bound tight around a rock. The mule took a step. Her hand begun to slip—there went the fingers! But still she kept hold.

Now she was stretched. "¡Tira! ¡Tira!" the Mexicans shouted. They laughed. "¡Está sumida en el lodo!"

Her head was back. She bit a piece of blue sky. The mule took another step. Strings of anguish pulled in Jensie's neck and shoulders. Then her fingers' hinges slipped; she was torn loose. "Daddy!" Jensie cried. She grabbed to a boulder. She nigh splintered her fingers as the mule took another step.

Now she was holding the rope with both hands. "¡Ahora mira la grullita volar!"

She would never never never never give up, let them drag her to death, but now she was running along behind the mule. The mule walked fast. Sobs of shame and rage broke in Jensie's throat. The rocks were mean to her feet. She bumped against a boulder. Stones and branches tore her feet, a hundred thorny things her shift. Now she tripped into a stumble that made her lean off-step.

She fell. She broke brush with her knees. She couldn't get up. The Mexican boy rode up on his horse. "¡Alto!" he said. "Desátala."

The mule stopped. Jensie lay panting on the ground. *It's so hard to die*, she thought. She wanted to die. She wanted to. But how lock out the everlasting breath? She was trapped by her own self. Pain put up a fence around her. Wouldn't she ever be free? Death. Everywhere, every minute, things come easy to it. Even small critters die. Why had it to be so hard for her? O the blood, it's a long worm that means to keep hold. The heart, it's tied in like a knot; the brain, it keeps on winding, winding.

"¿Qué, Bernardino?" Toral said to the Mexican boy. "¿Le tienes compasión?"

24

"No," Bernardino said. "Desátala."

Toral laughed. "Míralo," he said, "tiene miedo a la grulla." He and the Indian laughed.

"Yo la voy a desatar," Bernardino said angrily.

Toral and the Indian laughed. "¡No la dejes picarte las manos!" Toral said. Bernardino laughed.

Bernardino untied the rope from Jensie's wrist and shoved her up onto the mule, behind Toral. They rode up the canyon. Jensie hated them. All these Mexicans —this fat devil in front of her in the saddle, that mean, high-cheeked Indian riding along behind. And that boy too. She wished they were dead. She wished she was dead her ownself. And that's what she was going to do, too: she hadn't eaten since yesterday. And she wouldn't *never* eat. She'd starve herself to death first, days and days, with all her might. Until she dropped dead from off this mule. Or it come a night when those Mexicans would sneak up to do their mean business and find her dead—without a mind to her. Safe and cold.

All morning long the mule and horse climbed through the canyon. The canyon walls rose like mountains on both sides. It was nothing but rocks everywhere, and the canyon sides sometimes a dusty coliche rock, and sometimes here and there some short dry bunchgrass or a spread of yellow bitterweed. Once they passed a clump of canyon walnut. Once they seen a parchbacked rattler. That was all there was. Except that hot sun. Jensie kept the blanket pulled around her to hold off the sun.

After a long while the canyon sides begun to round out. The sky opened blue. Two specks of hawks pinned rings up under the sun, shedding their thin cries. About noon the horses topped a rise. And this was the queerest country Jensie ever did see.

Toral twisted in his saddle. His belly bulged out from the rest of him, hairs shiny blue on it. "Brasada," he said to Jensie, and pointed his thick finger in a circle. That country went on and on. Nothing kept it in but where the sky held it. It was mostly flat, with here and there a tiresome easy roll to it. There wasn't a thing growing higher than a man's head. Most of what there was wouldn't have come above a body's ankles, hardly. Sandbur and tumblegrass. If anything was green, it was that hard-skinned green against the hammering of the sun.

Toral grinned and leaned toward Jensie, a string of mulerabbit meat whitening in his teeth. "En esta tierra los hombres son libres," he said. Suddenly he spurred the mule. Jensie almost fell off. "Huchaa! Huchaa!" Toral shouted, and a deer started up sudden from the brush. Its white flag showed. It jumped over a bush. Its forelegs were up; its neck was stiff, it was that graceful. Toral reined in the mule. He laughed. "¿Ya ves, mi corazón?" he said. "Eso es todo lo que nos puede hacer daño."

They stopped for dinner and to let the horse and mule rest. The sun was awful hot. The horse and mule browsed on mesquite beans. Bernardino pulled a hank of tumblegrass and shook the dirt from it. He poured a mite of water from a gourd into the crown of his hat. Then he dipped the grass into the water and fed the drenched grass to the mule and horse. Those two critters couldn't get enough of that wet grass. Jensie heard them chomping the wet grass. She shut her ears against it. She sat under a mesquite and broke off thorns and tried to pin up the rips in her shift. Her face and legs where the blanket hadn't covered her were red from the sun. It hurt. Her gullet was dry as dust. But she didn't intend to eat. No, not ever. Nor drink, neither. Not a speck would pass her lips.

The horse and mule chomped the wet grass. The Indian—they called him *El Nahuatl*—fetched his serape blanket cupped full of hairy-skinned black persimmons from the brush. He hunched down and showed a persimmon to Jensie. He grinned. It made his scar wrinkle. "Chapote," he said. His voice came out a guttural noise from his gullet. But Jensie wouldn't take the persimmon. She drew her knees up and tried to back away from him. El Nahuatl pinched the persimmon between his thumb and forefinger, and the pulp popped out. He sucked it into his mouth. He wiped the black juice from his chin. Yesterday Jensie had swum in water. All that Nueces! El Nahuatl showed another persimmon to Jensie. But she wouldn't take it.

Then the Mexicans sat in a huddle near Jensie and smoked and ate parched corn and black persimmons and said Spanish and supped water. She wished they'd quit *supping* that water. They'd sup and talk, sup and talk, and blow wet smoke from between their lips.

Toral handed the gourd of water to Jensie. "Toma," he said. Jensie shook her head. But oh how her gullet ached for water! "Es buena agua," Toral said, and sloshed the water in the gourd. Jensie whispered *No, No, No*, and squeezed her eyes shut. It drew her burnt cheeks tight.

Toral turned to the others. "No importa," he said.

"Pronto va a echar el pico pa' atrás como un pájaro."

"La lagartija vive trescientos días sin agua," El Nahuatl said, a guttural clacking in his gullet.

"Ella no es una lagartija," Bernardino said. The other two laughed. Then Toral said, "Vámonos." They stood up and walked to the horses.

Jensie opened her eyes. The first thing she seen was three fat black persimmons lying on the ground by her wrist.

"¡Ándale! ¡Pronto!" Toral called to her from the blue coyote. In a rage, Jensie swatted at the persimmons with her hand. They rolled off through the dust. The dust powdered their black jackets. Then suddenly it felt to Jensie as if those persimmons were rolling through *her*, through her belly all filled with dust. And when one of them split into juice against a stalk of grass, inside her belly all hunger busted loose. But *no*, she *wouldn't eat*; no, no, not ever. And the next thing she knew, she'd pinched up a persimmon and popped it into her mouth.

Devil in the flesh! Jensie hated herself. She wished she would choke on those seeds. But now that juice was a key that turned the whole sky loose. The hurt for water flushed all through her. Yesterday! She'd swum the Nueces! All that water! Gushing and gushing!

Toral pulled Jensie up onto the horse. She was in a dry sweat. They rode a long way. The horse begun to rock. It rocked like a boat in water. Jensie hadn't known she was so *thirsty*. Fishes, they live in water. They breathe water. Moist flakes of fishes, fried. Test the skillet with cornmeal. *No, don't think on that!* Grated green corn, the milk of it. Cow's milk, to wet the hairs at your lip, for you to lick. *No, don't think on that!* O a green-grape pie, plums, grapes, dewberries! Jensie's head swum around and around. To suck marrowbones! Soups and juices! Rice water, hominy water, honey water they give you when you're sick! Her mama held up a spoonful of bone-broth to her lips. Her mama's hands looked so cool and white, and moved as if through water, and made her drink bone-broth. Swaller and swaller! Crush a juicy melon. Water down a batch of poor-doo, wet cornmeal cush— *no, no,* she had to keep *hold!* This was her grief to pass through, her river to cross over before she come to death.

> *Next big river I'm bound to cross,*
> *Next big river I'm bound to cross*

Folks dancing, drinking cider, cider. Lordy, the sun burned fierce. Lordy, she'd got a desert down her gullet. That persimmon had puckered her mouth dry. Jensie pulled her hair through her teeth. Dry. She couldn't spit free the ends of it. She almost choked. But the Mexicans rode right on. The sun busted down, cut Jensie's head to splinters. Her head in pieces swum around and around. Turkey, rabbit, quail, doves—all made into stews, to sup. To sup water. From a spoon, from a gourd, from a bucket, from a stump. Around and around and around, water squirting everywhere.

It flung her from the horse, onto the ground.

She'd had a fit. Now the Mexicans were trying to make her drink water. She didn't want to drink it. She pushed onto her side and coughed it up. Now she had the dry heaves. Her strength was drenching out of her. But she didn't want any water. She wanted to die. And was that her heart's blood she heard withering in her ear? *Next big river I'm bound to cross.* Yes, there was her mama, wiping her hands and tying on an apron. There was her daddy, putting down his ax a minute. There was little Dee. She loved them. And now their lips begun to move. They were telling her how to do it, how to die and be free. Now her own lips were moving, saying *yes yes yes yes yes.*

But of a sudden her eyes come clear. The sun stabbed through them. She felt her irises tighten like a fist. She squinted. She seen the Mexican boy. He was holding something to her lips. It was wet. It was bitter. But her mouth kept on sucking. Her gullet was saying *yes yes yes.*

She tried to knock that wetness from her lips, but someone was holding her hands. And her mouth kept sucking. Oh, what was the matter with her flesh, that it just plain balked to deliver her, that it reached out on all sides and ate and drank and aimed to live, as if it wasn't her choice?

It's so hard to die.

Bernardino took the chunk of cactus leaf from her mouth. He fed her mashed corn and ashes mixed with water. Jensie cried, but her gullet said *yes yes yes.* And that evening El Nahuatl stoned two doves. He gave one of them to Jensie. Bernardino set the dove and a gourd of water on the ground, close by Jensie. Bernardino never said a word. Then the Mexicans begun to talk and eat.

The bird was a small bird. The Mexicans had

cooked it brown, with specks of burnt all over it. Jensie
swung between eating and not eating. Then, when she
thought the Mexicans weren't looking, Jensie hunched
down and ate the dove. Oh it was tasty! Jensie hid the
bones—she didn't want those Mexicans to see that she
had eaten it—and drank the water. Then she felt
better.

That night the three Mexicans didn't trouble her.
Toral tied a rope to her ankle, and then to his wrist.
He wrapped himself in El Nahuatl's serape, and
Bernardino wrapped in his own serape, and El
Nahuatl just curled up naked near the fire. Then all
three went to sleep. Whenever Jensie moved, the rope
would wake Toral, and he would look at her. Jensie
tried hard not to move. She didn't want Toral to look
at her.

She was so awful tired. But she had her a plan. It
had to do with rivers—with finding one, and then running away to it, and following the river to wherever it
took her. But the sound of rivers and the sound of here
got mixed. Jensie heard the noise of coyotes, way off
in the brush. Nearer to her, the horse half stumbled,
weary. Then a bullbat swung back and forth above
Jensie. It was a flick in the night. *Peent. Peent.* It kept
Jensie from thinking. But *it* was free. It knew its own
way, even through dark. Jensie thought of bullbats
flying open-beaked for bugs above a dusky river. Tana-
gers and redwings flashed through the thickets. *O-ka-
leeeee*. Bird calls, everywhere. The sun rose for a minute on her mama's voice, and lit the river. Swallows
all over the sky. Jensie climbed her way up a willow,
her mama's voice calling her most like birdsong, and

swayed there atop that willow, above the river, about to fly free; she felt like she might do it. But then she woke. She'd moved her foot. Toral was looking at her.

Toral turned over and went back to sleep. The bullbat was gone. Jensie lay a long while watching the stars, pretending a hundred times that she was free. But pretty soon her eyes begun wandering among the stars, and scattering her mind every which way. She was so awful tired. Before she knew it, she was asleep. With not a dream to it.

The next day.

The four of them rode a long way through the brush. Underneath that sun. And it seemed like they were never getting anywhere. The country went on and on. At midmorning they come across a bear. It was a big black bear that sat up on his haunches and looked at them, like he wondered what business those strangers had here, in *his* country.

"Tira el mecate," Toral said.

El Nahuatl slid off the mule. Bernardino undid his lasso and begun to ease the mule through the brush after the bear. All the while, he was shaking out that lasso into a wider loop. The bear just sat there, watching—until Bernardino got too close. "Git away!" Jensie yelled at the bear. Toral pulled Jensie's hair. "¡Quieta!" he said. But the bear dropped down onto all fours and begun to lope. "*Huchaaa!*" Bernardino shouted, and chased off after it through the brush. At one place the mule took a corner that you'd have thought would throw Bernardino for certain. Jensie hoped it would. But Bernardino stayed on.

Toral stood in the stirrups. "¡Lázalo! ¡Lázalo!" he shouted, and got so worked up he begun dancing in the stirrups. Around and around went that lasso. Bernardino flung it straight. Then he turned the mule smart about and drew the rope tight. He had that bear onto the end of it.

Bernardino kept the bear moving, off balance. He dragged it up past Jensie and Toral. The bear was howling and clawing, and it would half make it up onto its haunches, and then get a leg jerked out from under. It was in a pure rage. El Nahuatl threw another lasso onto the bear so that three of its legs were roped, and snagged the rope to a shinnery oak. The bear couldn't get free. It snapped and snuffed and thumped and twisted. "Let him up!" Jensie yelled. Toral laughed and jumped from the blue coyote. He wrapped his serape around the bear's snout and held it tight. The Indian pressed his knee against the bear's free leg; then he cut the bear's throat.

The Mexicans and El Nahuatl drank the blood. They tied the carcass across the mule and talked to calm the mule so that he would carry it. The Mexicans put Jensie up onto the coyote and Toral climbed up in front of her. Bernardino and El Nahuatl walked behind, leading the mule. They went a long way through the bear's country. Finally they come to a canyon.

Toral climbed down from the blue coyote. He and Bernardino led the mule and the horse down into the canyon. The sun burned down. The horse's back was in a lather. His shoulder blades jerked in his withers as he worked his way down into the canyon. And

33

Jensie reckoned that if they'd had to climb down the *other* side of the canyon, they wouldn't ever have made it. That side was straight-up as a wall, like a knife had sheared it. The limestone was weathered; it was splotched with brush. There were small caves here and there along it.

But this side of the canyon was steep enough going. The coyote hunched down onto his hocks to make it. He and the mule were in an awful hurry. There must have been water down there, because those two animals were going fast. Their hoofs chopped against the slope, raising a dust. The Mexicans cussed at the horse and mule, but they just couldn't make them hold back. The critters kept scraping their hocks, and sending rocks banging down into the canyon.

Down in the canyon there were three big, yellow-leaved pecans. Then Jensie heard water.

The Mexicans cussed in Spanish against the animals and the brush. Toral got his belly scratched, and started kicking at the brush. He was dripping with sweat. His boot hooked and tripped him to sliding down the canyon side. Bernardino tried to help him back onto his feet, and all Toral gave him was a lick and a cuss for it. Finally they come to the bottom. Oh it was sweet to see that water, two springs of it squeaking from the rock, spouting one above the other, cold and clear as a piece of magic!

Jensie scrambled from the coyote. "¡Alto!" Toral shouted. He was so peeved and sweaty, he wasn't going to let anyone but himself have the first drink.

Jensie ran to the springs. The water reached out to her. She flung herself at it. She scattered a hundred daddy longlegs that were bundled and throbbing under the shelf. She drank and drank. She gagged on it. It was so cold and sweet it hurt; it strung her neck-bones; it ached in her chest. Jensie drenched her hair; she drenched her ears and mouth and nose and eyes and whole face. Toral cussed. He tried to drag Jensie back from it. Then what a kick she gave him. Toral let out a yell. *¡Diablos americanos!* But Jensie went right on drinking. She couldn't get enough of that water.

And when finally Toral did drag her away from it, it didn't matter. Jensie had drunk her fill. She rolled over onto her back in the leaves and busted out laughing. She was soaked with water. Her belly with tight with water. But she'd won that far.

Toral rubbed his shin where Jensie had kicked him. Bernardino come up to him, grinning, and said something in Spanish. It put Toral into a worse rage. Toral fetched up a pecan branch and shook it and sent Bernardino running behind a tree. You could hear Bernardino laughing behind the tree.

Toral roared like a bull. He hove his stick at the tree. He walked over to Jensie and stood above her. "¿Grulla brava, eh?" he said, angrily. Abruptly he reached down and poked Jensie in the belly. What a hurt that was! Then Toral laughed—a mean dark laughter, dark as his face. He walked on off, leaving pecan trees and the canyon walls and the far sky up there spinning around and around.

Jensie dragged herself to a tree. She lay down on the fallen leaves. She lay there all day, sick, hurting, wishing she was dead. But the Mexicans went on about their work. They didn't pay any mind to her.

35

That night Toral come to Jensie, easing to her like a fox. He was wild like a fox. And when he was done, he flung the bloody skin of the bear onto her. "Duerme con tu amigo," he said.

his here was her stone prison. The canyon walls rose up. Up there was the sky. Time went on overhead. Clouds passed on over, changing into winter. The trees dropped their pecans and then dropped their leaves, and left black branches like a ladder to the sky. No use to her. And it hailed once, and once it snowed—as if the roof had fallen in on her prison. The ground was queer and pale as the sky. But the springs never stopped pumping their water. The horse and the mule grew their winter coats. Breath showed like foggy stalks. Bernardino made Jensie some leggings out of the bearskin.

These Mexicans were bandidos. Jensie knew that for sure now. Because up in a cave on that cliffside there was sacks and boxes of stuff. What they'd probably stolen. Hardware and tools and cloth—bolts of

flannel, twilled cotton, brown drilling. There was one
bolt that was the thinnest, smoothest cloth. It changed
its colors from blue to green and back, according to
the light, and you could see right through it. It was
called *seda*. "Vamos a robar el Camino del Presidio, el
Camino de Herrera," Bernardino boasted. "We rob the
Presidio Road, Herrera's Road. El Camino del Norte, el
Camino del Sur. The North Road, the South Road.
They must pay through the nose: por sus narices."
Then Bernardino would poke out his chest and strut
around in front of Jensie and say, "¡Ay! ¡Somos
bandidos muy finos!"

Jensie had begun to understand their lingo. "Someday I will be rico, a rich hombre!" Toral would say.
"We will all be ricos. Mucha plata, sí. I will wear a high
collar (un cuello alto). Mis pantalones, they will be
split, for the silver botones. And the chaqueta: silver
botones. Sí. Sí. I will wear many shirts. Mi caballo, he
shall have the gold bit and los silver estribos, and the
silver saddle also. We will ride up and down las vías
de Coahuila. Señoritas, they will say: ¡Míralo, es un
hombre rico! I will be alcalde, ha ha ha!" Then he'd rip
out another page from *La Jurisprudencia* and roll himself a cigarro, and Bernardino would hustle to fetch
him up a coal. Toral would suck big breaths from his
cigarro and blow smoke out fancy through his mustache, his fat fingers tapping the butt. His chest shone
in the firelight, bright as the facings to a generalísimo's
jacket—dorado, un gran uniforme—and the little
silver crucifix flashed from its nest on his hairy chest.

He'd lean toward Jensie. "Ah, mi Grullita," he would
say, "you will be muy bella, eh? You will wear the long

combs and las finas mantillas. You will walk like la
Dama Española. You will have lace and muchos rings.
Anillos con joyas. We will live in Coahuila, in la
grande hacienda. ¿Mucho mezcal, mucho aguardiente,
sí?"

Then he'd wink. "Certain hombres, in Laredo, in
Presidio," he would say, "sí, in San Fernando de Bexar
—they want my goods; they keep mucha plata para
mí." And the fire would fall to chunks, and the cold
sneak in, and the mejicanos hunch down around the
coals. Way off, coyotes sounded—those thin critters
scraping through the brush, doglike, barking their
hunger and lonesomeness against the night. Jensie
wasn't any better off than those critters, she knew it.
At least *they* were free. And oh, she didn't want to go
to Méjico at all. She didn't want rings and laces at all.
But the night come on. And the mejicanos' talk
wound down to fearful things.

"¡Diablos americanos!" they would say. "¡Malditos
tejanos!"

"Muerte para los tejanos."

"They steal from us, we steal from them."

"It is *justo*."

"They kill mejicanos, sí? We shoot them."

"It is justo."

They would look at Jensie. "Ay, Grullita, do you not
grieve for us? In Tejas it is un americano behind every
bush."

"¡Cabrones! The last time, they shot my horse from
under me. A fine horse he was. And we brought back
nothing—nada!"

Toral would say, "But Dios sees, eh, mi Grullita? We

39

come on you. Sí. We say: is that a bird in el agua?
Shakes her tail like un pájaro! ¡Ay! ¡Ay! Ha ha ha!
She puts a feather through us."

And grin. "Ay, mi Grullita, no be triste. You are
worth the horse!" And laugh. Get to laughing something wicked. Get to touching her. And night come on,
rustlings in the dark like the wings of birds. And it
come another day and another night and another
day, day on day.

Grief hung so awful heavy onto Jensie. How was she
to live? She'd wake to another day. Winter. Her serape
crusted with breath. Even the sun was cold. Jensie
would stir up the fire and hunch down next to it
for hours, trying to warm herself, trying not to think.
Sometimes there were pieces of meat—venison or
rabbit or a turkey maybe—and Jensie would eat and
eat. What else was there to do, that could keep her
from thinking? Sometimes she poked around through
the canyon. There was a pond below the cliff, that
the two springs flowed down to; below the pond there
was nothing but dry rock. Jensie would sit beside the
pond, and skate rocks across the ice-crust, plinking
away the hours. Or build herself twig-houses. Or dig
in the leaves under the trees and fetch up a frozen-
husked pecan. She come to know that glass-eyed
coyote, and to talk to him. He was a prisoner too. He
might have been free once; he might have run great,
grassy places, somewhere. But now he knew the mean-
ing of leather.

Jensie fed the coyote winter grass and the bark of
willows. The coyote's breath blew hot onto Jensie's
wrists. Sometimes Jensie would warm her fingers un-

der the coyote's mane, along the blood-filled neck. The horse looked up at her out of his one good eye and Jensie, for all her own sore grief, felt sad for him. Then the horse would press himself against Jensie, as if he wanted her to know. She knew. She fixed his saddle sores. She rubbed the needles and skin off prickly pear, and put the green pulp to his sores, and the sores begun to close. But just about the time the sores would get well, the banditos would ride out again (one always stayed behind to keep an eye on Jensie) and that horse would come back all covered with his old suffering. "No importa," Toral would say. "It is his life. Such heridas, they do not hurt after the saddle has warmed them." But the coyote horse would look at Jensie with his good eye, and Jensie knew: the map of Méjico.

And there were other things to do in order to forget, or try to forget. Sometimes Jensie cooked. Sometimes she plucked a turkey or a mess of doves. Sometimes, if the mejicanos shot a deer or a bear, Jensie would cook some of it, even though Toral always took the best parts for himself. And sometimes Jensie would just plain press her head against the trunk of a pecan, and try not to think.

It hurt to think.

Sometimes, for whole hours, Jensie would stay in one of the caves where the bandidos had stashed the things they'd stolen. The floor in the cave was a yellow dust. The ceiling was black from when the bandidos had burned the mud-daubers out. Or maybe it was Indians who'd burned their fires here, turning their venison and chipping their flints for arrowheads and talking in their Lipan tongue. There had been Indian

41

deaths here once. Bernardino told her. A fever had come down, killing babies mostly; there were Lipano babies buried all over this canyon—their small red bones. Not so long ago. "Lipano, he does not love this cañon."

But Jensie would put her mind to other things. She played games with hinges and augers; she pieced herself together a brown, cotton drilling dress, picking the edges for thread and forcing it through with a catclaw needle. And she loved to run her fingers across the bolt of seda, it was so soft. It sent a ripple up her fingers. She'd think on other folks, other places. She'd wrap that blue seda around her and pretend the wildest things, things she'd heard tell of: white-skinned ladies under hung glass lights. Then of a sudden, her own hands would seem brown and ugly across that cloth, almost like a mejicano's. Jensie would just ease down to the dust and cry. Yes. Yes. If it weren't for her grulla hair, and her blue eyes, she'd *be* mejicano! And once Bernardino climbed up and seen her crying that way. He took her hair in his hands and wiped her eyes with it. But she turned her face away.

Jensie knew what Bernardino was about. He was just like the others. What were her tears to Bernardino? Her griefs weren't any more to him than the griefs of that coyote horse.

Bernardino said a word in Spanish. Jensie shut her ears against it. Bernardino made a sad face. Jensie shut her eyes to it.

Bernardino touched her. It froze her feelings cold. Because Jensie had learned a thing: the way women and women and women can come to hate. She pressed the back of her head against the rock, hard, trying to make it hurt enough to overcome his touch. The cold, burnt rock blacked her hair. Then Bernardino let go.

When Jensie opened her eyes, he was staring at her. For a long while Bernardino stared and stared, and he never said a word. Then he stood up and walked out.

For days and days after that, Bernardino never said a word. He'd look away whenever he saw her. As if he knew something.

Jensie bided her time, waiting for the chance to get away. If she could only steal that blue coyote and set his nose toward the Nueces. Or if only somebody would come, her own people, hunters maybe, and take her away. But this canyon was the dead center of nowhere, God forsaken. Jensie prayed and prayed, but nobody come. Just snow, once. And hail. And wind all the time shuffling past her, overhead. But one time, she had her chance.

It was toward dark of a warm day—the first day of spring, Jensie reckoned. It seemed to Jensie as if everything was trying to hold out this one last night, and when morning come it would bust out green. It put the fiercest grief in her. There were new birds in the canyon: scrub jays, and a pair of black-backed finches. These had woke her this morning. They would wake her again tomorrow, even more cruel.

The two finches sung across to each other, as Jensie walked in the canyon. *Tewyee tewyer* sung the two finches, hurting Jensie with their song. And beside Jensie the broomwillows were about to poke their buds

43

loose. Down by her ankles the rush grass had lost its crispness and was streaked green in the stems.

Around the edge of the pond, the last of winter's ice.

Jensie sat for a spell beside the pond. She poked black, icy leaves from the mush with a stick. Of a sudden she had the queerest feeling—as if, hung through the air, not coming from anybody, a hand might any minute brush her neckbones, rise spread-fingered through her hair. As if a wind of a voice was about to touch her. And those finches weren't singing any more, either. Jensie dropped the stick. She looked up. Way up there, at the top of the canyon, was an Indian. He was looking down at Jensie.

Toral was under the pecans. He called low to Jensie, "Get under the trees." When she got there Bernardino whispered, "Lipano."

The Nahuatl was up at the top of the canyon right now, talking to the Indian. Pretty soon he come back down. He spoke in Nahuatl. Jensie couldn't understand any of it. But the Mexicans begun to hustle. Bernardino hackamored the mule and the horse. He saddled the blue coyote. El Nahuatl threw corn and dry venison into a sack and filled gourds with water. Toral fetched ropes and the two guns.

"¡Grullita!" Toral said. "Go up into the cave—vete a la cueva." Then he pointed to the top of the canyon. "In that direction it is la región perdida." He pointed down the canyon. "That way it is el campo de los Lipanos. Indios. Do not go. ¡Vete a la cueva! We will be back." Then he began puffing up the canyon side, leading the coyote along behind him. El Nahuatl and

Bernardino followed after. The Indian wasn't anywhere to be seen.

Jensie couldn't hardly believe it. It was too quiet.
Any minute now a tree ought to split and start talking
mejicano. No, all she could hear was her own one
breath, and the blood pumping in her ears. *Tewyee
tewyer* sung the finches. O she had to get herself away
from here!

Jensie tied some corn in a kerchief. She filled a
gourd with water. She took a long drink from one of
the springs. She spread out her bearskin and rolled the
corn and watergourd in it and tied the bundle with a
thong. She listened. Only that toward-dark sky, overhead. One bird flew to another tree. There was the
splash of the two springs. That was all the sound.
Jensie started up the canyon side in a fever, the way a
moth makes for light. *Tewyer!* went the finches, as if
to nip her on her way. Jensie grabbed rocks and
branches to pull herself up. Sometimes the rocks
slipped from under her; she skinned her knees and
her shins. Her blood got so loud it hurt. At last she
come to the top.

Jensie ran. She was like a sparrow that's been put
in a box; when the top is let up, it breaks out in a
rush and tumble and flutter. Jensie tripped and
bumped her knees and snagged her dress on the
brush. But she got up, scratched and panting, and
ran some more. She didn't feel any hurt but the hurt
to be free. It was like a blind thing in her, beating its
wings. Finally Jensie couldn't run any farther—she
was lost in a cedar thicket. Her arms and shoulders

45

were so weak she hadn't the strength to push through. There was a cottony taste of dry blood in her mouth.

Jensie fell to the ground. Dry cedar needles sprinkled down about her. She knelt on her hands and knees and arched her back and gaped and heaved. When the spell was over, Jensie knelt there, trembling like a newborn colt, all weak and sick-smelling. Then a terrible weight begun to grow onto her. It pushed her down to the ground. Her fingers tried to flick against the weight. Her eyelids tried to flick. But it wouldn't let up. It kept getting bigger and bigger.

Jensie sank down under it.

When she come to, the night was one dark bruise above her. Jensie opened her eyes. Her eyes were filled with the dark. Not a star, even, to put sight into them. Then Jensie heard a low *snuff*. Something was scraping the ground close beside her. Jensie bolted upright. She heard the furry turn of some secret critter and the swish of it outward through the cedar. She sat up in a hurry. She stood up. She was still newborn-coltish in her knees. What was it that had snuck so close to her, bent on doing what? Jensie listened. She heard it moving around, out there somewhere in the dark—the soft, circling sound of some furry critter. And other noises: small peeps, scratchings, twig-shiftings, the midnight tumble of beetles (was it?), or the fretty hush of birds. Somewhere a clunk of antlers (was it?) against branches. Jensie begun to walk. She walked right on, through the full dark. For a minute every noise stopped except that soft circling. Then Jensie come out of the cedar. She walked. She hoped she was headed westward, toward the Nueces, where her mama and her daddy and Dee were right now. Sleeping. Alongside the Nueces. Were they hoping still? Were they dreaming right now of her? Now the coyotes begun to bark. First two or three, way off, in a low drag-out tune. Then suddenly, from right behind the next bush, it seemed like, come sharp yaps that scared the liver and lights out of Jensie. Then, from farther off, the sound of a whole pack of coyotes in a grief-muzzled chorus, their voices pitched just a mite higher than the last time. It seemed like not one coyote could get high enough but that another couldn't get higher. And then suddenly they stopped, listening for her. And then suddenly let loose one tall moan that seemed it would brush the clouds from the sky and set the stars free. When that didn't happen, the coyotes got bitter; they started rasping their songs one against the other. Then suddenly they stopped, listening for her. Then suddenly they let loose again. And that fur-footed thing was circling and circling Jensie. What was she to do? Her heart beat every which way, like a bat trying to sound where that circling was. And it was awful dark. Jensie felt her way with her feet. She stretched her hands out in front of her, against the brush. She kept on walking. She seen that if she'd stare straight blind ahead she could make out things from the edges of her eyes. But roots snaked at her ankles. Stones and splinter-sharp sticks cut her feet. Plenty of times she fell. Her face and arms and legs were scratched; her dress was torn. Her hair was tangled with stickers and cedar needles. Now a wind begun to blow. Jensie knew the signs of it, right away. It was the kind of a wind that has squeaked through such miles of stony country, distance has shaped it

47

cold. The scrubbed shanks of dead trees are the name
of it. The brush begun to creak, and then *bang* it was on
her. The wind was fierce cold. It threshed her hair
back; it gripped and thinned her dress; it strung her
with whiplash branches. Jensie squeezed her eyes
shut. She leaned through the wind to a scrub oak. She
pressed against the scrub oak and begun to untie the
bearskin. Above Jensie the oak leaves shrilled. From
deep inside the oak tree come the strain of oak mus-
cles. Then the hail beat down like fury. It strummed
and stoned Jensie and stung her head; it broke oak
branches. Jensie hollered. The wind hollered. The hail
banged down. Jensie covered her head with the bearskin, but then the hail stoned her ankles. She covered
her ankles and the hail stoned her head. And then
almost before the hailstorm had begun, it was done.
The hail stopped. The clouds passed eastward. They
let loose a full moon low in the west. Hail covered
the ground—miles and miles of it. The moonlight
stretched across everything, cold as a wet knife, and
struck jewels among the hail. Eastward, against a
sliding cloud, a queer rainbow showed: it hadn't any
colors to it: its arc was in different shades like the
changes of madness. And all around was the bright
empty air and the pebbled floor of ice. Jensie shivered, and not just from the cold. Stars were flung like
limedust through the sky. They hadn't any word.
And the moon never said a word. Just cold stones in
the sky. And the cold lost silent country was everywhere, everywhere, and Jensie's flesh was alone, single, in the middle of all this country, under all those
stars and stars and stars. What was the use of a
tongue now? Stones talk better. Or the use of a color

of eyes, or notions of flesh, or any sweet breath across a body's mouth?—dead bones talk better. Knuckle-bones. Moonbones. The everlasting bones. White. Things caught from moon-side. Albino eyes. Oh this was a fearsome craziness! Oh both ends of that moon-bow touched, and that was from never to never; was from never to never, and Jensie kept on walking, aching from the hail and the lostness. Alone. Above the faraway ghostly earth. It was most like a dream. She would lift up a foot, set down a foot. Her feet lifted so slow, set down so forever. And when catclaw and agarita scratched her, Jensie never felt it. She sat down and dragged up her stony-cold foot and pulled an inch-long cactus needle from it. It didn't even hurt. She tore strips of cloth from her dress and tried to wrap her foot. But she couldn't get her fingers to work, they were that cold. She tried to stand up, but she was too stiff. She had to crawl on her hands and knees across the hailstones until she come to a scrub oak. Then she pulled herself up. She hobbled from scrub oak to scrub oak, hoping westward. Somewhere along the way she'd lost her bearskin, with all the corn and water in it. But now Jensie didn't care. And then her blood begun to grow pale. Or was it the sky up there?

When the sun showed, it was in the wrong place for her.

Jensie walked and walked. The sun begun to take a strong hold. The hail-broken brushcountry steamed. The hailstones shrank. Jensie walked and walked. She come to a canyon.

Three black-branched pecan trees down there. And smoke threads winding upward from a fire. *Tewyew tewyer* sung the finches.

All that country. One long mean circle. And now here she was . . .

Oh God!

Jensie eased to the ground. She was too worn out to cry, even. She pressed her face into the dirt, among some bunchgrass. The tips of the bunchgrass pricked at her eyes, but didn't let loose a tear. Only let loose a low moan out of her.

> *Here we go round the mulberry bush,*
> *The mulberry bush, the mulberry bush.*
> *Here we go round the . . .*

Oh God!

Once she'd worn a scrubbed-clean dress and danced that, ages and ages back. She could hear herself singing. And went around and around until she fell to the dirt. And heard herself laughing.

Jensie opened her eyes. She stared at the dirt. She heard the Mexicans laughing in the canyon.

What had this country to do with her? There weren't a mind to cedar. The grass hadn't any fingers to care for her.

She heard the Mexicans talking in the canyon. She reached out with both her hands and grabbed to weed-stalks and stones. But these hadn't any comfort.

Well, it was those Mexicans or that country, one.

She took a deep breath. She pulled herself up. She was worn out, *plumb wore out.* But she pulled her innards back together. She listened to the Mexicans.

¡Humanos!

Then she begun to climb down into the canyon.

FOUR

The mule and the horse stood by the pond. The mule still wore the crosstrees the Mexicans had put on him the night before. The crosstrees had slipped around and under, and now they dangled from his belly—loose leather and cinches. When Jensie come down into the canyon, the mule didn't even look up, he was that woeful with those crosstrees troubling his belly. His head hung close to the water. His ears drooped in their misery-signals. The blue coyote looked up at Jensie, then lowered his head again until his whiskered chin just tipped the water, dripping small drops.

Jensie knelt by the pond. She ran her arms into the water up to her elbows. Her scratches stung. She drank some water. She almost fell into the water, she was so tuckered. She splashed water onto her face and

51

ran her wet fingers through her hair to rouse herself. The horse and mule stood stock still, their chins dribbling. Jensie pushed up onto her feet, through the weight and ache of herself, and turned toward the pecans, where the smoke was rising. The afternoon sun shone down on the naked trees and threw their black shadows to the ground, to the winter-blackened leaves. The Nahuatl stood at the edge of the trees, watching Jensie. He had a pile of sticks in his arms. Jensie walked up to the trees and past el Nahuatl to the fire, where smoke unwound from orange flux to spindle upward between trees—first a blue, then a pale, then the empty sky up there. Bernardino sat on the other side of the smoke, watching Jensie. He was wrapped in his serape. His face was dirty, pebbled with sweat. His eyes shone red from the smoke.

Jensie said, "¿Has comido?"

Bernardino didn't say anything; he only looked a long while at her. El Nahuatl dropped his sticks beside the fire. *Tewyee tewyer* sung the finches. That was the only word.

Well, Jensie wasn't going to waste any time. She went right to work. She was nigh dying of hunger. She got her coals in shape. She mixed cornmeal and bearfat and water in a gourd. Then she spread her coals and sprinkled them with cornmeal and shaped her mix into cakes and put them on the coals. She sprinkled them with cornmeal and covered them with coals. While they were fixing, she rinsed out the gourd at the spring and filled it with water. Then she propped the gourd near the fire and fished stones from the coals to drop into the water. In no time at all the water was boiling. Jensie plucked crisp dewberry leaves from canes on the canyon side; she stuffed them into the gourd and let them steep. She raked the hoecakes from the ashes and laid them out on a rock, black-crusted, smoking hot.

She sat down to eat.

"Hssst!" Bernardino said angrily. "*You do not eat!* I do not let you eat. It is no justo."

"I'm hungry," Jensie said in English.

"¡No es justo!" Bernardino shouted. Then he said, "Toral is dead."

Bernardino jumped to his feet. "¡Diablos americanos!" he said. "They *kill* him. El Escorpión está muerto. They shoot him in the face."

"¡Diablos americanos!" he said.

The smoke from the fire wrapped his legs; it wound around his serape and darkened his face. Bernardino didn't take notice of the smoke at all. His eyes shone red through the smoke.

Bernardino spread his malediciones. "¡Cabrones! ¡Malditos, malditos tejanos! Gringos. Perros—the white-faced dogs!

"This is not their country," he shouted. "Nosotros dominamos el Camino del Norte, el Camino del Sur. Pertenece a nosotros los mejicanos, no a los tejanos.

"El Lipano, he leads us to them. Lipano, he hates el gringo also. Sí, they have come to find us. But we fight. There are six of those gringos."

My daddy! Jensie thought. "Bernardino!" she said. "*Did one of them have yellow hair?*"

"No," Bernardino said. "But we kill two. It is una pelea grande—a great battle. But the others get away."

He said, "We go to rob the two dead ones, for they

53

do not need it. Toral, he is bending over un dead tejano, muerto—the dead one shoots him in the face."

"Ihuan chicome tlaminiloti," el Nahuatl said quietly, and fetched up a hoecake. "¡Maldito seas!" Bernardino shouted, "you do not give a damn." El Nahuatl looked at him. He shrugged his shoulders. He turned and walked to the trees.

"¡Muerte, muerte, a los malditos tejanos!" Bernardino shouted after him. He shook his fist. The leather-thonged crucifix swung from it. "¡Ojalá!" he shouted.

His voice hitched of a sudden low, like it was being jerked from him. "¡Heridas en mi lado abiertas por mis pecados!" he whispered. He shook all over, and the serape fell from his shoulders.

Bernardino was streaked with blood. His shoulder was black with blood. Proud flesh, like a mushroom, puffed from his shoulder. The black crust broke open. Bright blood dabbled through the pulpish fat, treble red branches among the dried black branches. Heridas en mi lado abiertas por mis pecados. *Wounds in my side opened for my sins*.

"¡Ay! ¡Ay!"

Bernardino slid to the ground. His body twitched. He made uncommon noises in his mouth.

His blood drenched the leaves. Jensie ran to him. She tore strips from her dress and pressed the wadded rags against the wound. Now she noticed the Nahuatl standing in front of her. She looked up at him. The Nahuatl just stood there, looking at her. Jensie stood up. "Llévalo a la cueva," she said to the Nahuatl. But she didn't reckon he'd do it. Then, for a wonder, the Nahuatl bent down and lifted Bernardino. He begun to carry Bernardino up to the cave. Jensie crammed a hoecake into her mouth. She took up the gourd of hot tea and followed after them. When she was up in the cave she said to el Nahuatl, "Trae unas hojas." The Nahuatl fetched in some leaves. He piled them in a corner. Jensie had him put Bernardino on the leaves.

Jensie tore some flannel from a bolt. There was a basket of salt stashed in the cave; Jennie thinned some in the hot tea and washed Bernardino's chest and belly. The wound had quit bleeding. Jensie cleaned around the wound and tore off new strips of flannel and packed it against the wound and wrapped Bernardino's shoulder. She had to lift Bernardino up to wrap his shoulder; when it was done it had worn her out, she was that tuckered. She sat back against the cave wall, panting.

She saw el Nahuatl squatting on his heels at the cave entrance, watching her. But Jensie hadn't the strength to be scared. "*Vete,*" she said. "Vete, vete; go away, go away." Then she eased down onto the leaves, and slept.

Bernardino was touching her face. Jensie sat bolt upright. She rubbed the crust of sleep from her eyes.

Evening had come on, sinking its darkness into the canyon. The Nahuatl wasn't anywhere to be seen. Outside, the three pecans poked upward like long black fingers through the dusk. Somewhere a dove was spelling night.

Bernardino lay onto the leaves and looked up at her. Jensie could hardly see his face in the half light. After a while he spoke.

He said, "Why do you come back?"

"I hadn't any place to go," Jensie said, in Spanish.

"Y yo también. And I also," he said.

"I walked, but I come to here," she said. "I was so awful tired."

"It is a big country," Bernardino said. He stared up at the ceiling. The edges of his eyes were white in the dark. He said, "Tengo quince años—I am fifteen years old. When I am twelve, I am walking in my town of Costeños. Soldados step from a doorway. They do not ask my name. They are the men of General Manuel Mier y Teran. They take me to their campamento, outside Costeños. Now I am soldado, they say."

He was quiet for a while. Then he said, "It is a cruel life, Grullita. We walk to Matamoros. Muchos soldados there. Toral is there. We walk the long march, a través del Río Grande, hacia Tejas. Mucho mesquite, mucho granjeno; many miles of dust. There is not much water. There is nothing to eat. But Toral teaches me. He puts his hand in the leaves of chapote, the black persimmon, his hand in the leaves of the plum, ciruela, and we eat. He throws a stone under huajillo; there, there is a rabbit. He plucks the dove like a grape from branches. Toral teaches me.

"Sometimes we come to a town. The people do not want us. But Toral teaches me. The chicken, he walks on two feet. Dios put the chicken there so that we may eat. We borrow the chicken, and Matrona does not miss it. And Dios breathed life into the pig: when we eat the pig, we eat God's breath. I learn to borrow the pig. How to choose the horse: praise the tall, but saddle the small. One time we choose two horses, and in the night we ride away. El Nahuatl is with us.

"It is very funny. They are the General's horses. But we are not caught. Ellos no nos alcanzaron.

56

"Ah, Grullita, comprendes? We are *free*. We shoot the deer. We take from the americanos what we need.

"¡Ay! Toral teaches me! And he could ride the horse. He was at one with the horse. It was the truth of the horse in his body."

Now in the graying light Bernardino's eyes were closed, thin-lidded, twitching as if in pain. They made his face seem so easy hurt. And his length seemed such a long and sunken thing.

"Toral is dead," Bernardino said at last. "Él fué como un padre para mí. He was like a father to me."

Suddenly he cried out into the dark, "Toral! Toral! Where have you led me?" He tried to rise from the leaves, but he fell back down. He held out his hands. "Look at my hands," he said. "My hands have been as two hawks, feathered against pity. I have worn my heart wild like the cat's. The snake has crawled behind my eyes and eaten my sight.

"¡Ay! But he has shaken down the leaves. And I have seen my death."

Bernardino lay back. After a long while he said, "¿Cómo te llamas? What is your name?"

"Jensie," Jensie said.

"Yensi?" Bernardino said. "But your hair is very bright. The wings of the white crane. Grullita. The little white crane. It is strange you have such blanca hair."

"I don't care, I don't care!" Jensie said in English. "I wish my hair was black."

"¿Blanca?" Bernardino said.

"I wish I was dead!" Jensie said.

"Yo no comprendo," Bernardino said.

"¡No quiero vivir!" Jensie said.

57

She heard Bernardino rising in the dark—the shift of the leaves under him, the sense of him leaning toward her in the dark. She was afraid. She pressed against the wall. She felt his hand touch her neck. She felt his hand move along her neck. It woke her again into that grief and rage.

"Why do you always touch me?" she cried.

His fingers in the dark, touching her eyes.

"I hate you!" she cried.

She begun to beat him. She beat sharp breaths out of him in the dark. But somehow his hand caught her wrist, and she would have opened her mouth to screech but of a sudden her body gave in. All the strength shook out of her. Bernardino pulled her to him and she moaned.

He held her. He begun to rock back and forth in the dark. All the animal fastness was gone out of him.

"I am wild, wild," Bernardino cried. "Ay, mi Grullita, heart of the white crane, breathe onto me. Cover my eyes. Breathe onto me. Think I am the wild horse, mesteño, so gentle me."

He said, "Al Río Nueces. I will take you to your home."

Springtime opened fine. Everything unlocking everywhere. Like this joy in her. The uncramping of pecans to bust a bud, tongue-thrusts, until the high pecan branches were flecked with pale leaves. And the poking to feather-tendrils of broomwillows, and the bright anguish of the bean-flowered redbud to be free. Grasses to break their crease. Dayflower, spiderwort, unfoldings of new world.

And up above, the streaked blue air.

Soon Jensie herself would be free. Bernardino had said it. What she had never counted on. She could cry sometimes for thinking on it, for thinking to be free, for touching her mama's face, for saying *Mama do you know me? This is Jensie.*

Or sing. Sing out like a bird almost. But the birds sung for her. The canyon begun to fill with birds, day in, day out, coming up from Mexico. *Ke-whirr*, the ashthroated flycatcher. Rock-wren's pipings. White-breasted nuthatch's *why? why? why? Teeyew teeyer* sung the finches, their breasts of yellow putting a color to the world, stoking a fever in Jensie until she sometimes moaned for thinking on it. Then she would stop whatever work she was at—tending fire or whatever—and walk under the pecans, beneath bird and leaf. Or run out onto the new grass, gasping from the hope in her.

And a scrub jay splotch blue the brush above her, *check check check check ke-wesh.*

In the broomwillows, redwinged blackbirds courting. Chittering. Stiffening their red-patch wings.

There were times too when Jensie feared Bernardino would change his mind. Then she would work harder than ever and try not to think on it. She took care of Bernardino. She dug the roots of *tuna* and washed them and mashed them on a rock. She put the mash to Bernardino's shoulder. The wound healed. Jensie baked Bernardino hoecakes, and sopas of venison. She made Bernardino take lots of rest so he'd get well. She hunted out the shoots of sour dock and careless weed and pursley beside the pond. She cooked them for Bernardino. She cooked him doves and rabbits and squirrels, and sometimes a turkey that the

59

Nahuatl had called down with the hollow of a bone. Then Bernardino would eat, and talk to her in Spanish. And Jensie would talk.

She would talk to him in Spanish, about her home, about how things would be, there, right now. Her daddy would be plowing the bottoms—it was that time of year. And Dee probably following along after, with a stick to set the corn. Jensie's chore, she told him, would have been to put the corn in and dirt it over. And she would tell him how her mama would be airing the cabin now, it being spring and all. Her mama would scrub the benches with ash-soap and set them out in the springtime sun to dry. But that would have been *her* chore, Jensie said, if she would have been home, and and and and, and she reckoned that that was what her mama and her daddy and little Dee were doing right this minute.

Because Bernardino was somebody to talk to. It felt good to talk. He listened to her. And he'd been stolen himself, from his folks when he was little, and so he knew how it was.

Bernardino wasn't much older than her. His self hadn't come yet to be a man's. He was thin-chested like a bird. He was beanpoled. He was even more beanpoleish than usual, now that he was sick. But if his arms and shoulders were smooth and olive, his face was already telling old. His face already had wrinkles on it, around the sad almond eyes. His eyes were always sad. Even if he smiled, it was a sad smile.

Once Jensie asked Bernardino why he was so awful sad.

Bernardino looked at her. He brushed his hair—

blue wing of the crow, *el cuervo*—back from his eyes. He said, "It does not matter."

But after a while he said, "You will go home, sí, mi Grullita? Your people will care for you. Sí, you will become the tall *Dama*. Your hair will shine in the light. It is what you wish. But I am of the dark. And already I am nothing. Nada.

"Onetime I think, soon I will be rico. Soon I will have money to carry to Costeños. But there is no money. Nada. And if soldados see me, I will be shot. I cannot go to Costeños. And if americano sees me, I will be shot. Nada! I am as nothing, and my death will show it."

Bernardino stared at his hands. He talked low, like he was ashamed almost. He said, "I think of the tall men, español, who come before us, who do brave wonders in the world and wear the silver coraza and the silver helmet, so that their walking shines. Conquistadores. Then it is good to be soldado. Sí.

"My mother, she is Spanish.

"And also," he said, "I am triste, sad, because I think . . ." but then he brushed back his black hair and wouldn't say it.

But she was going home. Soon. Bernardino had said it! And sometimes Jensie liked to be by herself to think on that, to sit on a rock in the springtime sun, maybe, and piece together the new yellow dress that she was sewing to wear to meet her folks. She had dyed the cotton flannel yellow with a dye made from the roots of agarita, the way Bernardino had showed her. Now she was sewing her dress, seeing herself in it over and over, meeting her folks. Or sometimes she would just sit in the new grass, beside the pond, and think on going home. She liked to listen to the blue coyote as he chomped the new grass: the horse would bite the grass and chew it crosswise in his teeth; every so often he would blow out breath to clear the grass from his nostrils. Or listen to him drinking water: he'd swallow slow; then, when he was full-up, he'd lip the top of the water and let the drops tumble, peaceable. Then suddenly Jensie would be in a hassle to put the crosstrees on him and light out across country. She'd proceed to light out across country a hundred times in her head. In no time at all, she would be looking down onto the breaks of the Nueces. Way off down in the valley would be the river, where she'd swum, where she'd gone one day with Dee to hunt pecans. Jensie could might'near reach down with her hand and touch the river. No, reach down a hand and touch her daddy's cedar-picket cabin and pop the roof off and say "Look who's here!" No, she'd *fly* down there, if she was going to be that fancy, and sit in the top of a chinquapin tree, and sing out for all the world like a bird flown up from Mexico to mention spring, and sing, sing, sing until her folks had to come out. "Listen to that there *bird!*" they'd say. And then she'd come running out from behind the tree.

Once while Jensie was lying in the grass strung out on such conjurings, a finch come shuttling above her in his silly dips, the way a finch does, all sprinkled with twirps. And Jensie didn't know why it tickled her so, but it did. She started laughing. She rolled over onto her belly and laughed into the grass.

Too much laughing. Why did her belly hurt so? So she just lay there, her hair making a nest in the grass, possessing her face. It ached in the small of her back too. But pretty soon the sun, pouring down, drenched away the ache and stroked her whole girl's-length, until her insides bloomed and she was floating in the green-smell and warmth.

That same evening, after Jensie had fed the blue coyote handfuls of new grass, and was walking up from the pond to the pecans, the Nahuatl stepped out in front of her. His thin-slit eyes. His crooked knit of scar. "¿Qué quiere?" Jensie said. What do you want? But the Nahuatl did a queer thing. He reached out his hand and touched Jensie's belly. Jensie turned and ran to the spring.

The Nahuatl didn't try to follow her. He stood where he was, watching through his thin-slit eyes. And Jensie couldn't help herself—she busted out laughing again. For no good reason. What reason could she have? She was afraid of the Nahuatl. And still she laughed.

He stood watching her. She was laughing and laughing. The laughing hurt in her belly. She begun to tremble. She stuck her hand in the water to stop that laughing.

The water was cruel cold. It had come from a thousand miles deep in the dark of nowhere, and it stopped her laughter. The Nahuatl walked over to the fire and sat down beside it, with his back to Jensie.

Nits and midges hung about Jensie's face. They made her sneeze like pepper. They made her crazy, wanting to laugh. A daddy longlegs bobbed upon his stilts. A scrub jay bounced into a redbud above her and shook down fierce bean-flowers to the rock, stirring the madness of a laugh in Jensie. What was the matter with her? God, if she didn't grab hold to some-

63

thing she was going to unravel into wild. Too much! Too rich! Too much hope, that's what it was. Ever since Bernardino had said he would fetch her home. Now she was sick to her stomach from it.

Jensie leaned against the wet rock. The shelf in front of her was hung with black-spined ferns. She grabbed a tight hold and heaved the clabbered laughter up.

Bernardino was standing behind her. "What is the matter?" he said.

"*I want to go home,*" she said.

That night Jensie had a troubled dream. It wasn't about the Nahuatl. She dreamt she was home, sí, and it was dark inside the cabin. The greasewick lamp had filled the whole cabin with smoke. And everybody was turned away from Jensie, busy at one chore or another, so that she couldn't see their faces.

But Jensie stood in the middle, in her dream, in her yellow dress, waiting for her folks to talk to her. They had their backs all to her. Finally her daddy stood up. Her mama looked over at him. Her mama was crying (if that was her face). But her daddy's back was still to Jensie. Then her daddy spoke. But he spoke in mejicano.

Jensie woke right up. "Daddy, Daddy, háblame," she heard herself say.

Jensie lay there wide awake. She couldn't get mejicano out of her head. It was all her thought. This rock, coliche; that moon, la luna; those trees, los nogales, palo blanco, el cedro, los olmos; this grass, that flower: sacaguista, huajillo, violeta; these hands, las manos.

Jensie looked at Bernardino, on the far side of the cave. He was asleep. En la luz de la luna—in the light of the moon—his face was white.

Jensie closed her eyes. Bernardino's face come clear, bleached by moonlight. Jensie opened her eyes and tried to think up Dee's face. But little Dee hid his face behind a bush.

¡Ay! ¡Ay! Jensie thought. *Se fueron de mí—they are gone from me.*

And the worst was, in the days that followed, Jensie couldn't for the life of her call up her folks' faces. Or if sometimes she did, it was like faces in a splintered mirror.

¡Se fueron de mí!

Because now all her thought was español. Oh, she grieved against it. But especially when she wasn't thinking, she was thinking español. And this changed the look of everything. At the sight of a tree, the words los olmos! or el nogal! pushed through her head. And hojas!—the stir of new green along branches, where el aire los perturbó.

Jensie's folks thinned away like ghosts. Jensie tried to call them back. But their foreheads were all splintered, their eyes all empty, their motions forced and pale. Even la casa, cedar-picketed, with the latch to the door of it, begun to fail, and a far woman to set her scrubbed benches distantly in front of it. Ay! They had darkened her—Toral, el Nahuatl, Bernardino. They had put a space between. And *he* had darkened her, El Furioso Sol, from way up there where he hung in his stretch of light. And time had darkened her tongue, until now it was talking español. Jensie couldn't help it. Only agua, cold and wet, tasted real in her gullet. Only los olmos, el nogal, el palo blanco to her eyes. Only the darkness of el Nahuatl obscuro; only Bernardino's face, oliva, almendra-eyed, triste, triste, real.

Even Jensie's hands talked español.

Hasta las manos de Jensi hablaban español.

But one day Bernardino said to her, "Mira el cielo —look up at the sky. It is going to rain. Thus. Dios is great and wise. He sees this country becoming dry and lifeless, though it is spring, primavera. He sees that el cañon looks like humps of crust with hot trees to it. He sees the deer in the brush, and they are so poor that their ribs stick out. Dios sees all this, and the sight grieves him. When Dios is grieved the brightness of the sun becomes dull. Thus. The winds cease to move. All things become brittle and as though they were covered with glass. The grass becomes still and deep-colored. Dios is growing sad. All trees and cañons look dull. They seem silent and heavy, waiting the will of Dios. Soon Dios weeps, millones y millones of tears that fall over llano and cañon, over buck and doe— tears that change the leaf and fill los hoyos, the holes-in-the-rock. That is how it is going to rain.

"Tomorrow, Grullita," Bernardino said, "it will be el tiempo-de-los-hoyos. The time-of-the-rock-waterholes. Then we shall go."

Following the big rain and the clear night, it was a heavy dew—the dead leaves black with dew and the green leaves tipping under the weight of it. And now morning had pushed up a thick fog from leaf-loam and inner kindlings of new grass.

This is the morning, this is the morning, ésta es la mañana, sí. Jensie walked towards the springs. The fog peppered her forehead and beaded her pale hair. Big drops sprinkled from the trees. Jensie could hardly breathe, she was so roused up. *This is the morning.* She hadn't slept all night. Each posture had been a new awakeness; the cruel ache of waiting had filled her skull. Now the prickling wet made her head ache the more. And the worst of it was, she felt sick to her stomach again, like the past morning and the morning before that. She walked through the fog with her mouth open, gulping breaths, the cool wet stinging her lips and creasing down her throat. That stopped the sickness some.

The brush showered when Jensie touched it. She couldn't see two feet in front of her. The grass where she stepped was heavy with dew; dew was caught in the collars of turkeyfoot; it was balanced in twists of tumblegrass and on the blades of grama grass and switchgrass; it wet the strings of panic grass. The dew doused Jensie's ankles and freighted the yellow hem of her dress.

For a minute the fog shifted: drenched pecan trunks, floating wet-black branches, a dripping shelf of hung limestone. Jensie seen the two springs. Then the fog closed back. But she come to the two springs easy, by way of habit.

Jensie knelt on the wet rock below the springs. The rock soaked her knees through her dress. She shivered from it. *This is the morning. This is the whole day, opening.* She breathed deep the wet morning, and it went all through her.

She listened. She heard the noise of the mule and

67

the horse down by the pond, and the cussing of Bernardino and el Nahuatl as they put on the crosstrees. Then the fog muffled the noises.

The fog peppered Jensie wet. The springs splashed down their water and sprinkled her. In the run, a square-stemmed mint bent, toppling its wet onto her wrist. A bird fluffed awake in the redbud up above and shook down wet buds and water onto her. But she didn't care. She craved the wet. She was awake. She was breathing. Only this puny sickness somehow down inside her—she couldn't figure why. But she wasn't going to let any sickness keep her back. She was going home. Ésta es la mañana, sí.

Jensie drank water to stifle the sickness. That felt better.

She brushed her teeth with a root of hackberry. She rinsed her face in the run, and wiped her face dry on her homemade dress. She pulled her wet hair back and tied it with a piece of flannel.

Now she was set.

She stood. She looked down at her dress. The yellow suited her. But her hands and arms seemed so dark. What would her folks think if she was to bust out into mejicano? Like she was thinking in right now.

Her lips tasted smoky.

The fog spread to bright: the sun trying to poke down through. The brightness hurt Jensie's eyes. The coyote whinnied down by the pond. "¡Grullita, vámonos!" Bernardino called. The fog thickened back to gray. That sun just can't make up his mind today, Jensie reckoned. ¡Ay! ¡Ésta es la mañana! she thought, and a shiver ran through her. Bernardino called again from down by the pond, "Vámonos." "Ya voy," Jensie whispered, and ran through the wet canyon to the pond.

The mule and the coyote stood by the pond. Their tails were long wet switches that brushed the grass. Their coarse winter hair, that they'd just begun to shed, was matted with wet. Streams of wet veined their barrel bellies; cowlicks of wet plastered their quarters. Their forelegs were plastered deer-thin with the wet. The crosstrees were on their backs. These were hung with strings of watergourds and serapes and sacks of smoked venison and such. A Mexican rifle, *mosquete*, was tied to each crosstree. Rags and skins had been flung across the crosstree frames to make saddles. The animals' reins dangled from their jaws into the dew-filled grass, which they chomped lazily, like they figured they were never going anywhere but just right here, where there was plenty of grass and water.

Bernardino, on the far side of the blue coyote, punched his knee *kathump* into the horse's bloated belly. The coyote flung up his head, farted, snorted, ran a few steps, but Bernardino was right along beside. The coyote's belly shrank to half the size. Before that horse could think, Bernardino had jerked the chincha tight.

For a minute the fog thinned back to bright. "It will be a hot day," Bernardino said. The Nahuatl, who was tying some gourds onto the mule's crosstree, grunted.

Bernardino looked up. He seen Jensie. "Buenos días," he said. He leaned against the wet flank of the coyote and watched Jensie. His face was a soft olive color from the wet. His hair was bedraggled as a rained-on black minorca's feathers. Jensie laughed to see it.

"¡Mírala!" Bernardino said, and he grinned. He walked his fingers stiff-legged like a bird across the coyote's rump. "Look!" he said. "She walks through water like the long-necked crane. Look. Amarillo. She wears the yellow legs of the crane."

"This is my yellow dress," Jensie said.

"*Escucha*, listen to her sing!" Bernardino said. "Her beak is full of minnows." He laughed. He put his foot in the estribo and lit up onto the blue coyote. The coyote, peevish, shifted under the weight.

"Siempre me estás embromando," Jensie said, pouting. Why did Bernardino always have to tease her?

Bernardino, grinning, rode over to Jensie. He looked down from the horse at her. A darkness crossed his face. "Grullita," he said, "where will you fly to?" But then he laughed, and snatched up the tail-end of her hair.

"¡Ayí!" he said, "she drags her tail through water, long feather of white."

Then he wasn't smiling any more.

He looked at her.

"Sí," he said. "Sí. It is la grullita. Azul. The closeness of the water is in your eyes."

He was very solemn. He said, "Conquistadores. They led their prisoners on chains of gold. Or silver. So it is said, and I believe it."

He let loose of her hair.

"Give me your hand," he said. "Put your foot in el estribo. Watch out for the rifle, mosquete." He helped her up behind him, onto the blue coyote's rump.

But el Nahuatl had hold of the coyote's hackamore. He looked at Bernardino and Jensie. "¿Nos vamos?— we go?" he said. His voice was dark and quiet.

"Sí," Bernardino said.

"Where are we going?" the Nahuatl said.

"Al Río Nueces," Bernardino said.

"No," el Nahuatl said quietly. "Vamos a *Méjico*."

"Al Río Nueces," Bernardino said. "And you shall have the mule."

"¡Maldito seas! What do I care for the mule? And do you think the woman is only for you?" el Nahuatl said. He said it quietly. "We will take her to Méjico."

"We go now," Bernardino said. He tried to prod the coyote forward. But el Nahuatl held the hackamore.

"Give me the jáquima," Bernardino said.

"We go to Méjico," the Nahuatl said.

"You will ride the mule."

"Sí," said the Nahuatl. "And will you keep the woman for yourself? ¿Y vas a guardar la mujer para ti?"

"¡Vete!" Bernardino said.

The Nahuatl pushed the coyote's jaw down against its neck. The horse blew breath, and begun to step back. The Nahuatl was grinning all the while.

"You are not Toral," he said to Bernardino. He looked at Jensie. "And a caged bird flies where it must."

Bernardino jabbed his heels into the blue coyote. The horse bolted forward, jerking el Nahuatl along with. Jensie nearly fell. Now the Nahuatl wasn't grinning any more. He had a knife in his fist. Jensie seen it.

"You are not Toral," el Nahuatl hissed. "¡No! ¡Tú no eres Toral!"

Bernardino prodded the coyote again, slapping a hand against its neck. With a grunt the horse swung against el Nahuatl. Bernardino kicked the Nahuatl's wrist. The knife flew to the ground.

"¡Abájate!" Bernardino said. Jensie slid from the horse's rump.

The horse nearly trampled her. She scrambled out from under and ran to a rock. She climbed up onto it. Now el Nahuatl had hold of Bernardino's waist. Bernardino bent over, trying to twist free from the Indian's grip. "I will kill you," el Nahuatl said. The blue coyote shied sideways. The two men fell to the ground.

The coyote snorted, trotted off a little way, started chomping grass. El Nahuatl and Bernardino churned in the grass, silent in the grass and fog. Leaves of wet grass speckled their bodies. The twist of the wet olive body, the twist of the wet brown body. Their knees and their elbows smashed the grass.

The coyote chomped the grass. Every once in a while he'd look up at those two men fighting. Then he'd go back to chomping the grass. Bernardino and el Nahuatl fought in the grass. There wasn't a word to it. And what could Jensie do but fear to watch? The men wrestled, chest to chest, fierce grass-printed bodies holding and then slipping and then holding again, in a tangle of slick arms and legs and knotted backs printed with grass. Flash of olive skin against wet brown skin. Belly-smack and backward smash of grass.

Eyes closed, teeth grinning, the Mexican and the Indian fought in the grass. The blue coyote chomped the grass. The Mexican and the Indian kicked, bent, twisted, thumped bodies, rolled toward the blue coyote. The coyote snorted and shied back. The Mexican and the Indian grunted, bit skin to let loose a slicker wet, red, hit and choked and grunted. Now from the coil of their work their breaths broke fast.

The Nahuatl was on top—or almost on top. His arm

was across Bernardino's neck, choking. Bernardino's head was back, his eyes sprung wide, his teeth biting for breath. The two men begun to wind down slow. Slow trembling press of the Nahuatl against Bernardino; slow dragging up of Bernardino's knees, between himself and the Indian, like some last contraction of a dying thing. Only Bernardino's fingers, on the Nahuatl's back, seemed alive, dancing, clawing, like they were in another world.

Bernardino gave a kick. He knocked the Nahuatl back onto the grass. Bernardino begun to roll toward the blue coyote. The Nahuatl found the knife in the grass. He turned to Bernardino. He was panting, grinning. The blue coyote shied away, but Bernardino caught hold of his tail. The Nahuatl crawled toward Bernardino. Bernardino pulled himself up to the blue coyote. "¡Vámonos!" Jensie shouted, and kicked at the air. Bernardino slapped at the coyote, twisted its tail. It snorted, white-eyed. Then it ran toward the pond, gourds banging at its sides, and splashed across the water, dragging Bernardino along with.

The Nahuatl climbed to his feet. He saw the mule standing beside a boulder, humping and scraping its gear against the rock. He ran to it and reached for the rifle.

GARRUMP! the mule honked. It scooted up the canyon to the trees, honking and banging its gear. Jensie hadn't known what she'd done until she'd done it, but she'd fetched up a stone and hove it at the mule, hitting it smack-dab. Now the mule was up there under the trees, honking its indignation from its guts.

The Nahuatl looked at Jensie. And Jensie didn't know why, but she wasn't scared of him at all. There

73

was a fierce rush of triumph all through her like some maverick sap.

The Nahuatl didn't waste any time. He headed for Bernardino. He ran through the water, knife held high swosh swosh swosh the pond collapsed where he stepped, and water-spatter.

On the far side of the pond, on a rock shelf slanting into the water, Bernardino had pulled himself up between the horse and the canyon wall.

The fog begun to pale.

The horse was skittish. Its withers shook. It kept edging along the rock.

Bernardino didn't pay any mind to el Nahuatl at all. He was trying to twist the mosquete that was tied to the crosstree, and to aim it. He talked to the blue coyote, trying to gentle it. He had got the mosquete half across the horse's neck.

The Nahuatl was halfway across the pond.

Wet smoke broke from the blue coyote's withers. The explosion rattled through the canyon.

The horse skidded from the shelf, flinging Bernardino against the rock.

The Nahuatl paused. One leg was straight out, lifted half in running; it made him twist in the water. Now he was aimed around to Jensie. Such a look of surprise onto his face. Then he sat down slow into the water, a trickle of red curling from his lips. Suddenly the fog turned monstrous bright. It hurt, it was so bright. Then the sun broke clear. Wetness blazing everywhere.

The Nahuatl blazing in the water. He tried to rise, drizzling brightest blood and water. "Motzla mitzto-caroa!" he screeched. It was like the screech of a hawk.

It sprinkled blood from him. But he eased back down into the water.

The Nahuatl sat in the water. The blood that the air and sun made bright streamed from his chest to darken the red cloud circling him in the water. It seemed to Jensie that he was laughing. But he wasn't laughing. He was coughing. Rings of red water widened from him. The Nahuatl settled to one side, coughing. Slowly, as if the air was too much weight onto it, he lifted his arm and wiped it across his nose and mouth. It come away red.

Ay! Was he grinning a red grin at her? Jensie covered her face. But "Motzla mitztocaroa," she heard the Nahuatl say again—only this time quiet.

Jensie looked up. The Nahuatl was fumbling in the water and pushing back up and fumbling. He slumped slowly sideways into the water. He turned. Then both hands were on the bottom of the pond, fumbling. The Nahuatl's back shone bright, streaming its red in the sun. Now his face was barely above the water. The water wanted him. It was easy kin to his blood; now his body too was slipping into it. And if the Nahuatl seen the water, still he let himself down into it, easing down into it, and then down under. Where he must have settled. Bubbles pricked atop the water. The water quieted. The sun shone. An awful silence was everywhere, but for the two springs singing, and the noise of the blue coyote: back in the grass again, chomping. In the middle of the pond the water darkened like a thunderhead. Everywhere else it was stalks of light, sprung from water-seeds through the whole canyon, or was it Jensie's eyes that made her see it that way? The fierce

75

wet was on leaves and rocks and grass and watergourds
and the horse's flanks and leather: bright.

Jensie ran around the pond to Bernardino. He was
lying on the rock shelf. "Bernardino! ¿Estás bien?—are
you all right?" she cried. "Are you hurt?" "No mucho,"
he said. Jensie cried, she was so glad he was safe. She
well nigh kissed him, she was so glad. She well nigh
did. She held him to her. Bernardino said, "We will go
now, Grullita." Jensie helped him to his feet. He said,
"I do not wish to look at the water."

But he *was* hurt. His shoulder had opened. Jensie
fixed him up. Then they caught the mule and the horse
and led them up the canyon side, through the scrub
brush and scrub oak and cactus and steaming rock.
They climbed from moist hot bush to moist hot bush,
pulling the two animals up to the broad country and
the sun-packed sky.

They were panting when they got to the top. Bernardino especially. They rested. Then they were glad
to ride the mule and the horse.

FIVE

En español.
In Spanish: Ese sol tan alto,
esta eterna tierra. . . .

That tall sun, this forever country. Country of the thousand thorns. You can't walk anywhere but what you. Agarita, catclaw, mesquite, Spanish bayonet, tasajillo, prickly pear. That whole section-full over there. I'd hate to have to ride through look at all those yellow cactus flowers! They only open when the sun.

Where the shrike pins his lizards to a thorn tree. But we haven't heard or seen a bird all morning. Is it the air too heavy? How ever could they *sing*? Only rattlers live here. Scorpions under the rock of noon. They sting themselves when it gets too hot. Too hot. Wet. Wet fog this morning—don't think on that then you won't be thirsty. I can't *breathe*. Night is when things breathe around here. Yes, but water, that whole pond full, red —*oh don't think on that!* The scarlet flower of the barrel cactus: cacto viznaya.

You've drunk too much water already. Bernardino says. Can't hardly see, my eyes are so full of sweat. It drips. I'm wet all over but I don't taste salty.

Well, look at him up there on his blue coyote. His ankles wet with sweat. Beargrass hat, and that old cotton serape that his mother onetime made him. The cotton glares. Bernardino, here I am talking to you only you don't know it. Bernardino, Bernardino. Hunched above your blue coyote like it was the heft of the whole sun. Does he hurt? He hasn't said a word but once all morning. Is it still morning? No, that sun's Oh! that hurt my eyes! straight up there. Look at this white flower in my eyes now it's blue o sunflower now it's made my whole dark purple.

Feels like we've been riding *years*. Too hot to think, even. The ground down there. Hot. Limestone; chalky flint. How can a thing *grow*? Black sunspot down there in my eyes: skims the ground like a bird.

Listen to this mule's hoofs. Flint-splinters. That's how come this morning he limped. Poor mule. But he doesn't seem lame now. Poor mule, you've got a lather. Beaks, stingers, thorns, claws, prickers. This cruel country.

Last night I dreamt.

O Bernardino! Never *see* you more?

Whatever will you do when you go to Méjico? Whatever will you do when you go to Méjico?

He is good to me.

Oh this new thorn in me! What I hadn't known yesterday.

I don't want.

Ahhh, my arms, my neck, they're about to melt from the sun.

In the middle of this forever country. Yes, and somewhere under all this sun—but under trees somewhere —it's my folks, it's the River Nueces. But here. Bernardino. Him and me. No, my folks don't know the sun, like . . . Bernardino, sí, cover me with the shadow of your hand.

Because this tall sun.

But then, by late afternoon, they rode into another country. For a stretch anyway, though it was still the tall sun. But here for a space the grass grew. It felt queer to push out of the scrub and to ride into the open grass, but that's how it was. Jensie couldn't figure it. And flowers? She'd never seen so many flowers for to tell the spring. The sun kept a full hold, and spelled out what things might grow: colors of the sun and sky: blue windflowers and blue sage and yellow niggerheads and sandflax and a prickly poppy and a blackfoot daisy whose eye is like the sun. Only here and there a stand of scrub oak or mesquite to hold a sunshade to the grass.

The mule's hoofs swished slow through the flowers and grass. Tumblegrass. Curly mesquite. Look! A doe, with her fawn all speckle-spotted, ran through the grass. Then stood there watching them. But this forever country.

A little way farther the blue coyote quit. It was the hot sun. And the mule quit too, as if the sun had yoked him to that same hot tongue. The horse and mule, now that they were stopped, drooped their heads

79

and dripped lather and barely breathed. The heat wrapped itself around them.

The ache of not moving, of not stirring somehow this hot smother in her, was more than Jensie could bear. "Bernardino," she yelled. But it seemed like the air would hardly part. It seemed like Jensie could hardly push a word through it, it was that thick and hot and dead.

Bernardino didn't say anything. He just sat there, slouched above the blue coyote.

Jensie gave the mule a kick. She gave it another kick, and she gave it another one, too. Finally the mule heaved his weight across the grass, through the thick air.

Jensie said, "Bernardino? What is the matter?"

Bernardino said, "I can go no farther."

"Ay, Bernardino, let me help you!" Jensie said. Bernardino was about to fall from his horse.

Jensie slid to the ground and ran to him. Bernardino swayed above the blue coyote. He blinked back the sweat and looked down at Jensie. His face was nearly white, like a squeezed fist. He was gripping the crosstree so tight with his fists that the white knucklebones showed. Dark bruises shone all through his face, where the Nahuatl had walloped him—the swollen flesh backed and packed with the inner, hurt blood.

Jensie reached up to help him. "We should have stayed in the canyon," she said.

Bernardino straightened. "We could not have," he said. "But it does not matter."

"Sí," Jensie said. She understood what he meant: the Nahuatl—oh don't think on that!

"He follows me," Bernardino said. "He waits for me. And sometimes I think, that is his eye up there."

"Don't think on that! Don't think on that!" Jensie said.

Bernardino pointed. Way off yonder there was a low rise and a stand of mesquites. "But there are los hoyos," Bernardino said. He slouched forward. Jensie caught him. He grabbed her hand. "I am not well," he said. His voice was queer and dry. "Forgive me," he said. "It is not the sun. It is the many blows. But we have come to los hoyos."

Jensie led the coyote to the mule. She climbed back onto the mule. The mule drooped with the heat. Jensie looked at the rise. The heat stood up from the grass like a wall. Way off yonder, the stand of mesquites shook in the heat.

Jensie's eyes ached with the brightness.

She beat the mule with the coyote's reins. The hot air burned her naked, lifted arm. She beat the mule and he took a step and Jensie beat him and forced him through the heat, to plod through the grass and suffocations. She covered her arm again with her serape. She tugged the coyote along behind. It was a slow, poke-along hitch. But when they neared the rise the horse and mule grew eager.

They come to the rise. This was a monstrous slab of limestone as flat as a table. It stood hardly two hands high above the ground. All around the edge of it, it was burnt black, as if there'd been fires. The dozen or so mesquites—new greenish-yellow leaved, and sprung now with their creamy spikes of flowers, up like candles—ringed the rock and gave it some shade. All around the rock, the grass was cropped close: there were plenty of deer droppings. A scattering of yellow huisache daisies grew under the mesquites. These flowers hadn't been cropped. The deer at night had trampled them, though. The bitter, pinched smell of the huisache daisies put a sharpness to the air.

Bernardino said, "These are los hoyos."

Then Jensie seen. There was water in the rock: a honeycomb of potholes, hoyos, all different sizes, rounded and smooth-cupped. Years and years and the scarcest fingers of rain in this country had coaxed them from the rock. And last night's rain had filled them partly full again. In the potholes, old mesquite leaves and pods of beans had turned the new water to coffee color.

"Please," Bernardino said. "'Help me down from the horse." Jensie slid from the mule. Her kneebones and shinbones and anklebones ached from the shape of the mule. It hurt to walk. But she was glad to stretch.

The mule poked his nose toward the potholes, snuffing. Bernardino said, "No, do not let him drink." Jensie tied the two animals close-nosed to mesquites. Then she helped Bernardino.

Bernardino eased to the ground. He grunted. He sat under a mesquite. He laid his head back against the trunk, his eyes closed, the sweat puddling in his eyes, his neck lined with dirt and sweat. Jensie wished she could help him. Bernardino made a noise. Jensie knelt beside him.

"Do you want some water?" she said.

Bernardino shook his head. He said, "Do not be angry, Grullita. One day, two days, I will be well. Then

I will take you to your home." Jensie brushed the sweat from his eyes with the edge of her serape and wiped his face.

"I wasn't thinking on that," she said.

Bernardino flinched beneath her touch.

"I am sorry, Bernardino," Jensie said.

"It hurts a little," he said. He opened his eyes. "You are not angry that we must stop and rest here?" he said.

"No, Bernardino."

Bernardino tried to smile. Jensie looked at him. He was only just a boy. He said, "Sometimes when I see you, I think: she is like the doe. Sí. She means no harm, and eats the berries of agarita and what grass Dios gives, and permits the winter and the sun and the hunter's knife. It is in your eyes," he said.

He touched her. She stood up. Bernardino said, "It is painful to be the hunter, do you not see? You have crept to the deer. You must lie down by the roots of cedar until your heart becomes still. Dios watches. You point the mosquete. You shoot. And do you possess the deer, or does the deer possess you?"

The blue coyote whinnied. Bernardino said, "Grullita, lead them to the other side of el hoyo. Do not give them water until their necks are dry. Ay! It is odioso to be useless."

Jensie unloaded the mule and the horse. It was a chore. Bernardino tried to help her, but she wouldn't let him. There were black swatches of wet on the animals' backs where the crosstrees had been. Their sores had begun to open, too.

The coyote whinnied. The mule honked. They were ornery for water. Jensie led them to the other side of los hoyos. She hitched each of them to a mesquite. The mule and horse snuffed for water, and honked and whinnied. Jensie couldn't let them have any, though, because they'd get the founders for sure.

Jensie pulled up grass. She curried the mule's and horse's backs with the grass and put dust on their sores. This eased them some. She curried the foam and caked salt from their flanks and necks and bellies. She felt sorry for them. Their heads were hangdogged in a puzzlement of crave and waiting, the way a horse does. But pretty soon Jensie would fetch them some water.

There wasn't any breeze. The mesquites were still. The water was hot in the hoyos. On the far side of los hoyos, Bernardino had tied two corners of a serape to mesquites, trying to make a lean-to. Now he was setting rocks all along the back edge of it.

Bernardino looked across at Jensie. He tried to smile. "Come under the shade," he said. "We will hide here like two lizards." Those are the deer's eyes, Jensie thought. That brown hurt.

Jensie watched Bernardino's hands move, thin and silent, deerlike, as they set down the rocks. Even when you walk, she thought, it is with the deer's thinness.

Bernardino. Here I am talking to you, only you don't know it.

She walked back on around the rock. Bernardino had crawled under the shade of the serape. But it didn't look cool there either.

Jensie said, "Bernardino? Why is the rock all black?"

Bernardino said, "Look up in the mesquite—the six-branched one who shades the great hoyo. Do you not see it?"

"Sí," Jensie said. She hadn't noticed it before. Up in the highest branch of that big mesquite there were

84

deer antlers, tied together with beargrass. It looked for all the world like the bony, bleached nest of some other-country bird. Old turkey feathers were woven among the points.

"It is the sign of Lipano," Bernardino said. "This is his hoyo de agua."

Jensie looked in every direction. No, she didn't see any . . . But still . . .

Bernardino laughed. "Do not fear, Grullita," he said.

"Come rest in the shade, and I will tell you," he said.

Jensie crawled under the serape lean-to. She lay down. Under the serape, it was just as hot as outside. It was stifling.

"Lie still, Grullita," Bernardino said. "Soon you will be rested. And tonight a breeze will blow. That is how it is in this country."

Or a Lipano come on us, Jensie thought. Was it going to be a full moon tonight? Because that was when the Indians did their prowling.

Bernardino said, "This is the spring, primavera, sí? The Lipano is not with us. In the fall, otoño, when the grass has let down its seed and deer are strong from so much grass, then the Lipano comes. He comes from el norte. He takes what deer he wishes for his purpose, for there are many deer. Then he burns the grass. That is why the rock is black. Fire kills the thorny ones—cedar, agarita, granjeno—and makes the earth rich. And in the spring, as now, while the Lipano is en el norte, a few rains come. Then there is water in los hoyos, and much new grass, and the deer increase; and Dios speaks his pleasure in the many flowers."

Well, she was glad to hear it, Jensie said. Bernardino laughed. Then for a long while they lay there, not say-

ing a word, and the sun going on west. Jensie felt
somewhat better. She tried to figure the weave in the
serape above them. Bernardino's madre had woven that.
Once Bernardino had told Jensie how he used to love to
watch his mother at this work, when he was little, and
how his mother would sit so straight, and wear combs
in her hair, and tell him stories, when he was little.
Stories of the fox, the eagle, the ringtail, the snake.
Nowadays, did his madre think of him?

Jensie said, "Bernardino?"

"¿Sí?"

"Soon I will be home."

"Sí."

"Where will you go when I am home, Bernardino?"

After a while Bernardino said, "I do not know, amiga.
Shall I go to Méjico?" They were quiet a while longer,
thinking. Then Bernardino said, "This is the country of
death. But have you noticed? There are no flies here."

Of a sudden Bernardino said, "Motzla mitzlocaroa."

—The Nahuatl lifting from the water. "Ay! Do not
think on that!" Jensie said.

Bernardino said, "He speaks in Nahuatl."

"Yo no comprendo," Jensie said.

"It is best that you do not comprehend," Bernardino
said, "for we do not wish to talk of it." But later he said,
"*Motzla mitzlocaroa.* He means to say: *tomorrow it will
fall to me.*" Then Bernardino said, "Sí. I have seen my
death."

Jensie sat up. She looked at him. "Why do you always
think on that?" she said.

Bernardino's eyes were closed; his mouth was open
wide, bruises swelling the edge of it. He swallowed. Sí,

he was just a boy, no older in the world than her, as afraid of things as her, and scared like any other. "You do not understand," Bernardino said. "It waits for me. It is the Great One standing in the air. Its hand is over me, like this serape. I see the death of a bird and that is its word to me. And Toral. And el Nahuatl, sí. ¡Ay! ¡Ay!"

"Bernardino!"

"I am nothing. Nada."

"Shhh, Bernardino, no one will hurt us here," Jensie said. And after a little while Bernardino said *Sí*, and was quiet.

Toward dark, but while it was still the last of light, Jensie watered the mule and the horse. They drank deep and slow. Then Jensie let them out onto the prairie and put them in hobbles.

West, a low shelf of burning light, clouds, the last, like an orange-hot anvil; east, the first stars showing, and night rising like water to douse the anvil. The night was halfway across the sky.

Darkness everywhere. Jensie watched. And in her that feeling of waiting, like she used to get sometimes, for instance when it would be still midday and yet dark and the darkness set to rain and she would be waiting for the rain. Now the dark begun to spread across the prairie. The long, low, last of light. Jensie seen deer watching from the prairie, ghostlike, standing in wonder to see her at their watering place.

Back under the lean-to, Jensie and Bernardino drank water and ate strips of dried venison that the smoke had made salty. They mayn't build a fire, Bernardino said.

They could rest here and drink the water of los hoyos, "which the mesquites guard and the stone makes sweet," but they mayn't build a fire. "That is for Lipano only," Bernardino said.

And now it was night and the full dark. So many stars. The sky seems closer in Texas. What are all those small noises? Yes, it's—Jensie thought of the deer standing around on the prairie, waiting.

Soon a breeze come across the plateau. It stirred the mesquites and shook the serape. Jensie and Bernardino slept.

Jensie opened her eyes. It was morning. The deer were gone. The quiet, the white and first hush, was upon the grass. No birds sang in these mesquites.

The morning lay in Jensie's belly like a round stone. That sickness again. Wouldn't she ever be rid of it? Wouldn't she ever be her own self again? And *distance! distance! distance!* her heart, waking, cried—*and loneliness.* And if last night the sky had seemed that close, this morning the distance stretched everywhere. Only Bernardino here beside her, breathing.

Tall, empty, the sky, she thought. Not the speck of a bird across it. The empty spaces.

She turned to Bernardino. Sí, he was awake. He had been awake before her. He had been watching her in her sleep.

The bruises on his face were going down some.

"Do they hurt, Bernardino?" Jensie said.

"It is much better," he said.

"The swelling has gone down some," Jensie said.

Bernardino grinned. He said, "I can see out of my eyes now."

Jensie spread her serape on the ground, between them. She fetched venison and a gourd of water and set them out. "Gracias, Señorita," Bernardino said. "Buenos días," he said. Then they ate the venison and drank the water.

Jensie chewed on the salty meat. "I wish we had a green-grape pie," she said. "I'm tired of smoky meat."

"I do not know el grin grep pie," Bernardino said.

"You take a lot of grapes and a lot of honey and mash it and make yourself a green-grape pie, and then you have yourself a green-grape pie."

"That would be good," Bernardino said.

"I'm sure hungry for it," Jensie said. "Well," she said, "here's you a green-grape pie." She handed Bernardino a chunk of venison. They laughed and chewed the meat. But now the lean-to begun to fill with light. It was the sun. Jensie and Bernardino rolled over onto their bellies to watch it rise.

Rey.

The King of Everything. *Nos maravillamos de ti. We marvel at you.* Wherever do you spend the night?

And now here he come, El Furioso Sol, lifting up from Alabama or Mississippi. Had lit rivers. Had woke eyes. Had got the roosters crowing in Mississippi. But this here was his own country.

They watched the sun rise.

The pink sky. The paleness of newer light. The ground all black, still clutching the nighttime in its roots—such dark distances! Then the peep of fierce purple cap, and slow bulging up, like hottest blood. Jensie sucked in her breath.

Sí, we know who you are, Bernardino whispered.

It seemed for a spell like the earth would hold down

89

the sun. But the sun poked up through the black crust. It wasn't *round*, yet. It was a fiery little knob, brightening, loosening back the black earth. It bulged more. Now it looked for all the world like a redskin wild plum —if it was to bulge one bulge more, it would streak out its purple plum juice. But it did bulge. Bigger. It was crammed with bright, all swole. And it didn't bust, either. It stoked its fires to orange and then to white. It stepped out of the earth. Oh it was too fierce now for eyes, too cruel in its singleness. Jensie covered her eyes. But still El Furioso Sol stabbed through: the orangeness between her fingers. Or plum juice. Right through the skin. Only her fingerbones kept dark.

Jensie peeped out between her bright fingers. There was still a blackness down in the roots, the last settlings of night. What was that? It felt for a minute as though the land had taken one big breath.

The sun knocked the darkness from the grass.

It was the day. It was the whole light.

It was the distances. And when she come to her folks, would they ever again know her?

Jensie lowered her head against the dirt. The hot sun was in her hair. She smelled the heavy smell of the dirt. And already the heat was pressing the crushed huisache daisies. One lay petal-scattered at her cheek, bruise-leafed. Such bitterness! Would her folks be like strangers when she come? Would her folks count her from another country? Because she wasn't who she used to be. Who was that little girl once who was called Jensie, one day beside a river, one day beneath pecans? Lost! Lost! A splintered mirror!

Bernardino said, "What are you thinking, Grullita?"

Jensie shook her head. The crushed huisache daisy. The stink of bitterness.

Bernardino said, "I know. You do not need to tell me."

Jensie sat up. She swallowed back the bitterness. She brushed her fingers through her hair. Way out on the prairie the mule and the coyote stood, the sun onto their flanks, their long necks down, browsing the last coolness from the grass.

Jensie pulled back her hair. She felt the piece of flannel hanging half loose in her hair.

Her mama—the way her mama used to stand, staring out the door, twisting an end of hair in her finger. No she mustn't think on that, mustn't think on that.

Jensie got the flannel ribbon loose, but it was knotted and tangled with pieces of her hair. Bernardino said, "I will unknot it for you." Jensie tossed it to him. She held back her hair while he unknotted the ribbon.

The sun, climbing, shone into the serape lean-to. Jensie turned her back to it.

She held her hair. She squeezed her eyes shut. She would think on other things. Anything. "Where do the deer go, Bernardino?" she said.

"In the day?" Bernardino said.

"Sí."

"They lie down in the brush."

"Do they have un lugar favorito—a favorite place?" Sí. Talk to me. And that one beneath pecans—what hands she'd moved, what words she'd talked with—was another, different person.

"Sí. Sometimes. They like to lie under cedar. Under el cedro they are as the brush, and you cannot see them. And the day is best for their sleep. By day, in this country, things are very still. Thus in his sleep el venado can hear what moves to harm him."

Jensie felt Bernardino's hand at the back of her neck. She let him tie the flannel.

"Early in the night, comprendes?" Bernardino said, "There is the breeze. Then the deer can walk silently. Also at night the grass is cool to eat."

His fingers tugged her hair, trying to loop the flannel. "No te muevas," he said. He had to start over.

Jensie laughed. She pulled against his fingers. She had a good mind to tease him. "No te muevas—don't move," he said again. Jensie giggled. Bernardino ran his fingers through her hair and grabbed tight to it. *"¡No te muevas!"* he said, and laughed. And Jensie laughed. She was gone wild herself. *O Bernardino, gentle me. Cover me with the shadow of your hand.*

Finally Bernardino got the flannel looped. "It is like tying water," he said. Then he said, "Ya está—it's done."

"¡Ya está! ¡Ya está! ¡Ya está!" Jensie said. They both laughed.

Abruptly Jensie stood up. She said, "Now I will tend the horses."

"Today I shall do it," Bernardino said.

"No," Jensie said. "I want you to get well."

Bernardino said, "Señorita, you are a hard lieutenant."

Jensie crawled out from under the lean-to. "Beware of El Furioso Sol," Bernardino called after her. Jensie caught the horse and the mule. She gave them some water from los hoyos, and tied them under the mesquites. Hot as it already was, you'd have thought the horse and mule would be switching their tails against a power of flies. But like Bernardino had said, there wasn't a fly buzzing anywhere. And if it was a country of death, like Bernardino had said, it was a clean country. Swept by sun.

When Jensie come back to the lean-to, Bernardino was under it, toying with a mess of stones.

"What are all those stones for?" Jensie said.

"Grullita, look!" Bernardino said. He showed her the stones. "You and I. We play the game, eh? I teach you. It will make the day as short as in winter."

"There's enough stones there to fill a rooster's craw," Jensie said.

"Gallo is luck," Bernardino said. Jensie looked at him. He smiled. "You tease me," he said. "Come," he said, "play the game. It is a very fine game. It is the game of la pájara."

"¿La pájara?"

"Sí. The game of the bird. The crowned one. The one who runs along the ground. Corre camino."

The roadrunner. Coming out from San Antonio. Her daddy's face. ¡Ay! Her daddy sitting so strong beside her on the wagon. And that brown bird skittering long-legged from under Ginger, running as fast as most birds fly. What's that there *bird*? she'd said.

Some calls hit roadrunner, Honey. Some calls hit chaparral cock. I'd like to hitch it to this yere wagon. Git up, Ginger!

To the River Nueces. To the River Nueces.

Oh a splintered mirror!

Bernardino said, "Come. I will teach you to play. I would like to teach you."

Jensie looked down at him. He was watching her eagerly. She hadn't ever noticed that red speck caught

93

in the brown iris of his eye before. She seen herself in his eyes. She knew then that that was who she was.

Bernardino said, "Why are you sad, Grullita? Do not be sad." He leaned toward her. He touched her wrist.

Jensie sat down beside him. She said, "Sí. Teach me the game, Bernardino."

"¡Sí!" he said. "¡Sí! It is a very fine game. Look!" he said. "It is of my own doing. I thought it up myself."

"I couldn't ever do that," Jensie said.

Bernardino said, "Sometimes I am alone, comprendes? The army is stopped. We are waiting, waiting, waiting. One cannot weep forever for what is lost. I am sitting beneath a saltbush, comprendes? There is nothing to do. Nada. But there are always stones. I say to myself: I will make a game of stones." He threw his head back. He rocked backward and forward, as proud as a green-necked rooster. "It is *easy*," he said. "I think of la pájara, who is alone. I think of la víbora, the snake, who is not her friend. I make a game. Sí. I will teach it to you," he said. "You will be the first to know."

Jensie laughed. "Sí, I will play," she said.

"Watch," Bernardino said. He held up two stones. "This is la pájara, the bird. This is la víbora, the snake. You know how they are enemies." He held up a third stone. "This stone is the stone for rolling, do you see?" Jensie nodded. She took the stone. It had a mark on one side. Bernardino said, "That is the eye of la pájara, one scratch. I mark it myself." He turned the stone over in her hand. "Here are two scratches, do you see? It is the sign of la víbora, when he bites."

Bernardino stretched his arm out onto the ground. "La pájara wishes to fill her nest with eggs, thus—." He took three more stones from under his palm and

94

stuck them between his spread fingers. Jensie laughed.

"Why do you laugh?" he said.

"It's so many *stones*," she said.

"Sí," Bernardino said, "it is un juego muy ponderoso
—a very weighty game." They laughed. Bernardino
went back to parsing out the game. He was proud
of it.

"But la víbora wishes to eat la pájara's eggs, comprendes?" he said. "It is according to how the stone
throws. Sometimes la víbora comes to the nest, and
then I fear for la pájara. Sometimes la víbora eats la
pájara's eggs or kills her. It is according to how the
stone throws. But sometimes la pájara fills her nest,
comprendes? Then she is joyful. You will be la pájara,"
he said. He put a stone in her hand.

They played the game. Jensie put her stone beside
Bernardino's elbow, like he showed her. Bernardino put
his stone on the other side. Then they jumped their
stones—pájara, víbora—across Bernardino's arm and
wrist, according to how the dice-stone rolled. It was the
high sun and the long morning and the close smell of
huisache daisies and the clicking of stones and crossings of their wrists as the stone rolled. Sometimes
their wrists touched, crossing with stones. But Bernardino won the first game, because his snake had eaten
all the eggs. He won the next game, too, because his
stone come to the nest first, when there weren't any
eggs in it, "and that kills la pájara," Bernardino said. He
was making up new rules, Jensie said. No, Bernardino
said, for she could see it must be this way. He just
wanted to win, Jensie said. "Sí," Bernardino said, "sí,"
and started laughing. Then Jensie grabbed the dice-
stone and threw it six times straight, without letting

Bernardino have a single throw. Bernardino was roaring with laughter. But Jensie jumped her pájara-stone right up to the nest. "I win," Jensie said. "Two eggs do not fill a nest," Bernardino said. "Well, she's already *laid* the third one," Jensie said, "you just won't let go of it from your fist."

She dug under his hand for her stone. Bernardino wouldn't let her have that last stone. He was laughing. Jensie jerked at his fingers; that just made him laugh harder. She butted him with her head; then, while he was laughing, she worked the stone loose from his fist. "I win! I win!" she said again. She was laughing her ownself.

But that hot sun. So they rested a mite. Bernardino rubbed his shoulder where Jensie had butted him. "I am sorry, Bernardino," Jensie said. Bernardino said, "No tiene importancia."

After a spell Bernardino said, "Hyensi?"

"¿Sí?" Jensie said.

"That is your name?" Bernardino said.

"That is not how to say it."

"Yensee?"

"No," Jensie said.

"Heyensee?"

Jensie laughed.

"Chensee? That is your name?" Bernardino said. "Chensee?"

"*Jensie*," Jensie said.

"Chensi."

Jensie rolled over onto her back, laughing.

"Chensi? Chensee. No. *Je*-yen-si."

"¡Sí!" Jensie said.

"Jeyensi. Ay, that is very hard. We have not that sound in español. Jen-si. Jensi. That is your name?"

"Yes," she said, "that is my name.

"Jen-sie," she said.

"Jen-si," he said.

Jensie rolled over onto her side to look at him. "Yes," she said, "that is my name."

Then they lay a long while quiet, staring up at the serape. There wasn't any breeze. There was only the shade of the serape lean-to to cover them. The serape seemed to lift with the heat. Once a black-backed beetle come crawling six-legged across it, making its upside down way. Every two beetle-miles or so it would reach out and feel in the air with a slow, hard-shell puzzlement of its legs and feelers. "¡Vete!" Bernardino said once, when it hung straight above him. "¡Vete! ¡Vete! Go away." Finally the beetle come to a corner. It seemed grateful to get there. Then it was gone on around the mesquite. And the sun moved like a fire-shelled beetle along the tent of the sky. And sometimes Jensie and Bernardino slept, they were that drowsy, and sometimes they played la pájara, or talked, though it was too hot to talk much. And sometimes they ate the smoky venison and drank water.

Toward evening, the two of them walked out. They watered the mule and the horse, and hobbled them to browse in the grass. Then they went walking through the grass. It was all so quiet. It felt good to be up and about. The sun went down. The grass streaked Bernardino's and Jensie's ankles with its held warmth. But as they walked, the grass begun to cool. The first of a breeze stirred the grass. It cooled Bernardino's and Jensie's faces and bodies, and stirred Jensie's hair. Now the sky was all gray toward night.

Bernardino said, "Listen." He stood stock still.

Jensie said, "I don't hear anything."

"Listen," he said.

Coo-uh-cuck-coo, who cooks for you? The song was strung out like the tag-end of a thread through the grass. La paloma, the dove. The white-wing.

Bernardino smiled. "There it is," he said.

They found the nest. A dove, brown-gray as the dusk, white on her wings, beat up from the nest. The nest wasn't much more than a stash of twigs laid flat onto the ground. Two white eggs were in it, curled around with specks of dusky feathers. The eggs were bright, and perfect in shape. "Don't touch them," Bernardino said. "If you do, she will not come back."

But carefully, without touching a thing else in the nest, Bernardino fetched up an egg.

Jensie gasped. "You shouldn't have done that!" she said.

Bernardino held the egg, white in his dark palm. "You are weary of venison?" he said.

"I don't want it," Jensie said.

"It is my gift, and the gift of la paloma."

"There weren't but two," Jensie said.

"It is for Jensi," Bernardino said. "I wish Jensi to have it. What else can I give? And birds and animals must give to us. This is as Dios Himself has commanded. So do not be sad, Grullita."

He put the egg in her hand. She held it. It was still warm with the bird and life of it.

"It is for you," Bernardino said.

Then she knew she would eat it. She was hungry to

eat it. She was gone wild, that was what it was—just like Bernardino. She carried the egg back to the lean-to. Bernardino showed her how to open it. He chipped off the small end of the egg with his thumbnail.

"Suck it," he said. He held it to her mouth. Oh it tasted good! and she was gone wild.

"The dove will live," Bernardino said. "Dios watches the dove." He set the empty shell carefully between the angle of a branch and trunk of a mesquite. "It is my gift and the gift of the dove," he said. He pushed his hair back from his eyes.

Jensie said, "Gracias, Bernardino." Then Bernardino lay back. He seemed joyful. "It is well," he said.

The stars come out. The sky was clear and close as ever. That white eggshell shone, up in the mesquite, like a snagged star. Bernardino and Jensie looked up at the stars, the million pinpricks in the night. Jensie could have reached her hands up, almost, and stirred those stars, they seemed that close. Like stirring shiny flakes in the black settlings of a spring.

Bernardino said, "In the heavens all things are the reverse of here. On earth all things are seen only by day. But in the heavens all things are seen only by night. They are covered from sight in the day."

He said, "Look at the North Star, Grullita, where no bird can reach it, no matter how strong its wings."

"I see it. I could almost *touch* it."

"Sí. But it belongs to Dios. And do you see also the Great Wagon that guards la Estrella del Norte? It circles backward. It drags its tongue behind."

"Big Dipper."

"¿Qué?"

"It is what they call it."

99

"Americano?"

"Sí. For drinking agua."

"That is strange. It does not look like a gourd."

Jensie smiled. She could see his face in her mind's eye, and how he looked while he puzzled it. She watched his faces, inventing all the different ways of Bernardino.

"But if, as we say, it is the Wagon," Bernardino said, "do you know what I wish?"

"No, Bernardino, yo no sé."

"I wish, this one night, that it might move forward, in the manner of earth."

"¿Por qué, Bernardino?" Jensie said.

"That we might have this day again. Para que pudiéramos tener este día otra vez."

Flickings of wrists; crossings of stones; white shell of the dove's egg, broken, broken, broken in her throat.

She said, "Sí, I do wish it."

After a while Bernardino said, "Jensi?"

"¿Sí?" she said.

"Where did you live when you were una niña?"

"En Misisipi." That seemed a long way off.

"I have not heard of that country. Is it like Méjico?"

"There are many trees there. There's a big river."

"In the north of Méjico, we do not have many trees. But there are mountains. And in Costeños, where I live, there are fields. They are on the sides of mountains."

"In Mississippi they have to cut down the trees to make fields."

"Misisipi," Bernardino said. "I would like to know of it. ¿Es americano?"

"Sí," Jensie said.

Bernardino said, "Sí." And after a while he said,

"And someday Tejas will be americano. But now it is mejicano."

They stared up at the stars. Jensie could hear the mule and the coyote browsing on the other side of the hoyos. She didn't know why, but the sound of those two animals browsing put a grief in her.

Jensie said, "What will you do when you go to Méjico?"

"If I go to Méjico," Bernardino said. "And shall I go to Costeños? The campamento of the army is there. They will remember the horses of General Manuel Mier y Teran. Shall I go to Coahuila? Shall I work on el rancho grande? Maybe someday I will *own* el rancho grande, eh?" He laughed. It was a bitter laugh. Then he said— so lonesome his voice seemed to come from a long way off—"Costeños." Then he said, "But before all this, I would like most to learn to read, as my uncle could. But when I was little, comprendes, I had to work in the fields, and so I cannot read. But I would like to learn to read."

"I can't read either, Bernardino," Jensie said.

"They say there are many fine things in books, Grullita," Bernardino said. "They say that men have taken ink, tinta, and put down many strange things in books, and I would like to know of them."

"I don't know what I want to do when I get home," Jensie said.

Bernardino said, "First, Grullita, you will grow, sí? You will be la bella dama. Sí. Do not say no. And people will wonder at you. You will wear combs in your hair. And three layers of dresses, with many colors to them. Men will do as you command."

"I don't care about that!" Jensie said, "I don't want

that! Oh Bernardino, what shall I *do* when I am home? What will you do?"

Bernardino said, "I will think on you."

To have this day again!

Bernardino said, "When first I see you, I think: she is like a white bird lifting from the river. It hurts to see you. You are like la grulla, the crane, when she hears the hunter. She stands a moment still. She listens everywhere. Her neck is very tall and beautiful, and wet from fishing in the water. Her legs are long and beautiful and wet, and down about her feet her whiteness fills the water. Soon she will fly. That is how I will think of you."

"I don't want to go home," Jensie said. She was about to cry.

For a while Bernardino was quiet. Then he said, "You must."

"I'm afraid to go home, Bernardino," Jensie said.

She heard Bernardino turning in the dark. She felt him watching her from the dark. She swallowed, to keep back the crying.

"Why are you afraid?" Bernardino said.

"They will not know me. I do not know myself."

"You are La Grullita," Bernardino said.

"Sí," she said, "sí," and felt a stinging wildness in her eyes. Bernardino touched her wrist.

"You are Jensi."

"I do not know who I am."

Bernardino squeezed her wrist tight. It held back her tears. "You are Jensi," he said.

"¡Sí! ¡Sí! And what will you do when you go to Méjico?" she said.

Bernardino held her wrist. But now he was stroking

her wrist gently. She let him do it. He said, "I will think of you."

She said, "I will think of you." Because this new thorn. Because what she hadn't known before. Because what had come out of the dark of her, like black thorn from the dark branch of plum, and hooked to her, and hooked her to branch and leaf and flower. Black thorn, white flower. The cruel and loving tree of it.

He held to her wrist. He said, "Today I do not care about the world. I would like to stay here forever, Grullita. Jensi! ¡Mi Grullita!

"But tomorrow comes, and los hoyos dry, and we are not like lizards who can hold water in their tails. You must go home."

Jensie shut her eyes. She seen his face, behind her eyes, and it was wild and it was gentle. That red speck in his eye, where she lived. O Bernardino!

What will you do when you go to Méjico? I will think of you. I will think of you.

Ay! And was that *her* voice, of a sudden in the dark, all cracked among the dark? It sounded like the noise of a hurt rabbit. Bernardino squeezed her wrist.

He said, "Jensi!"

"¿Qué?" she said. The strong of his hand around her wrist.

He was leaning above her in the dark.

"Jensi," he said.

"¿Qué?" she said.

He was saying Jensi, Jensi, Jensi on her eyes.

"¿Qué?" she cried, "¿Qué? ¿Qué? ¿Qué?" and for a minute she was afraid. But there come a catch in her throat. For the sake of him. For Costeños. For his eyes. For his hands so awful slender. There come a catch in her heart. Then she flew upward to him, or him to her, while her arms gathered what they never had before.

It was his mouth to her ear lighter than any wind might blow from the tongues of summer to stir a hundred parts in her. It is your ear too small for my heart to bear. Here behind your ear where I cannot see it, mi corazón, it is pardusco, the mouse's color. Here where I kiss in front of your ear, it is too white. It is the wing of the dove. It hurts me. This is your face, she said, mi corazón. How shall I kiss your face? he said, for it is lighter than ash and might fall so. O it is lighter than the ash of los olmos, mi corazón! These are your hands, she said. Give me your lips, that I might speak, they said, mi corazón. You are another country, he said. Taste my hands, she said, are they different from yours? Have they more bones in them than yours? It is your body, he said, it is your mind, it is your heart, it is where you come from and where you shall go. My love is in my bones, she said, if you can find it.

So that he spelled her with his lips, to a grief of tenderness.

Mi corazón.

He was laughing above her in the dark: bright, broken, racking laughter that shook him convulsively.

"¡Muerte! ¡Muerte!" he cried. "There *is* no death. There *is* no death. There is *no death!*"

She held the weight of him, his trembling gone, his face to her neck, while this great womanly calmness grew over her.

SIX

This here was the breaks of the Nueces. They had ridden a long way along the ridge, with that canyon always off down yonder. Then the other side of the ridge had begun to slope. Here, where those two canyons come together, it was the breaks of the Nueces.

Somewhere behind Jensie and Bernardino, a morning's ride back, the plateau had lost its tightness. It had begun to roll. And farther back than that, yes, ages back, this had brought an opening for the weather. The weather had dug in slow, ages and ages slow, and caused a slope which caused a gully which caused a canyon. That is how it must have begun, Jensie figured. And then those canyons had commenced to dig in deeper and deeper, always headed south. Now, down in the deepest places, it showed the limerock to its bones. The rock lay in long naked slabs, the way Jensie reckoned God must have put them, in the Bible times, slab on slab. And in some places there was a long washboard row of ribs, along the bottom of the canyon, like some stony-footed mountain lion had clawed it. The noon sun brought out the pales and yellows of the rock.

Jensie sat on the blue coyote, and Bernardino sat on the mule. They looked down to where the two canyons come together. The dry-bed canyons. Then Bernardino and Jensie looked southward, where more and more and more canyons come together—all stone and shallow dirt, and splotched with brush—to be the Nueces. But to Jensie it seemed more like they were sparse-backed mountains instead of canyons, away off down yonder to the south, and that here she and Bernardino were on top of this tallest mountain of them all, and the plateau behind them was the top of the world.

And somewhere yonder to the south, past where Jensie could see, a valley would be opening wide, full of trees and a river, and that was where her folks were.

They rode down into the canyon. On the way down, Bernardino shot a turkey. Jensie hadn't even known there was a turkey there. All her mind had been set on getting down into that canyon—the horse onto its hocks, and every step a jolt to Jensie, and a jerk downward. It was hard work. Then that rifle had sounded and nearly scared the liver and lights out of her. But from right under a laurel bush close by come a squawk and gargle and thumping thrashing of feathers.

Bernardino ran down to the bush. "¡Mira!" he shouted. He dragged up a gobbler turkey. It was a big one. It was still thrashing. Bernardino let it down onto the ground, keeping hold of its legs. It flapped some more, stirring up all kinds of dust, and then flapped some less, and then its wings slacked; the bluish purse of its eye closed, and it was quiet.

Bernardino hefted it up. He could hardly lift it into the air, it was so heavy. Its wings spread out loose, bronze and barred. Its neck swung naked-headed, wrinkled blue near the ear pans. Its red wattles drooped. It had old grandpap whiskers on its breast.

Bernardino laughed. "You are weary of venison, Jensi?" he said.

He fetched the turkey to Jensie. "It is for you," he said. The blue coyote shied away from it. Jensie got down from the saddle and quieted the horse. Bernardino cut a hank of hair from the coyote's mane and tied the turkey's legs together. He hung the turkey from the crosstree, on the coyote's blind side.

They rode down into the canyon. The turkey swung below Jensie's knee, pushing its dead heat and feathers at her, its shingled legs a rasp of golden-scale against the crosstree. The turkey's dead toes curled upward. Now its hulk was without any use for it, and it hung heavier than ever it could fly. Its barred wings widened lazy-fan, its gold-tipped tail spread careless, and the vent loose-holed. The whole skin of it sagged, easing its feathers loose and mussy. As it turned in the sun the feathers changed to green and bronze and purple. It was a heavy bird.

Bernardino and Jensie rode down into the canyon. They rested a spell, and drank the last of the water. Then they rode a long way down the canyon. The mule and blue coyote picked their way deer-footed across rocks and between boulders. The canyon walls rose like mountains on both sides. There was nothing but rocks everywhere—long stone slabs and boulders and sometimes a dusty coliche rock. Only here and there was some bunchgrass or a spread of yellow bitterweed. Once Jensie and Bernardino come to a clump of canyon walnut. "¡Espera!" Bernardino said. He reached out and pinched the leaves of the midget walnut.

"Un momento," he said.

Jensie rode back up to him. Bernardino climbed from the mule. He commenced pulling up rocks from the dry creekbed. Jensie got down to watch him. "What are you doing?" she said. Bernardino's fingers were wet. "Agua," he said. From under the ground, into the hole he'd dug, come water. It wasn't much water—just a smidgen trickle of it. But it begun to fill up the hole. The blue coyote whinnied.

Jensie tasted the water. It was as sweet and clear as if it had been squeezed from the deepest, stone-coldest places. Jensie was sure surprised. "How did you know there was water here?" she said.

"The leaves of the walnut," Bernardino said. "They are very oily."

They drank water and lay down to rest together against a rock.

It was good here. It was peaceable. The afternoon trickled down about them. The rocks were so quiet and peaceable. Up in the midget walnut the leaves were quiet. The mule and the horse hung their heads, resting. Jensie watched the sky easing across. She was filled with the quiet. Up in the canyons somewhere a grasshopper buzz: peaceable.

"Tan azul," Bernardino said.

"¿Qué dijiste?" Jensie said.

"The sky up there," Bernardino said, and pointed. "How can it be so blue?"

"Right now my father is out working the bottoms," Jensie said. "That same sky." After a while she said, "I don't know why I'm so all-the-time hungry."

Bernardino jumped to his feet. He grinned. "I will cook the turkey," he said. "We will eat the turkey here."

"I thought we would get to my folks tonight."

"Sí," Bernardino said.

He said, "It will be dark then, Jensi."

Dee! Hush! Rufus, there's somebody at the door. Then her mama staring at her through the greasewick smoke, wondering who she was. That's how it would be! Jensie was scared. Scared. She knew it. And the closer she come to that cabin, the worse scared she got. Whatever would they think of her? Would they at all know her?

What would they think of Bernardino?

Bernardino said, "There is grass here, Grullita. There is water, and wood for fire."

She loved him, that was all there was to it. She loved the way he talked, hungering from the whole life of him. And how his hands asked and touched and put down and lifted, moving (like right now! see?) from the loom of his mother's fingers. But she guessed his eyes were the eyes of his daddy, the way the color would darken in his eyes when he was sad. She loved the darkness in his eyes. And how he'd push back (see it!) that old drag of hair from his forehead, and sometimes smile. And laugh sometimes—sometimes laugh like morning, like pulling back the covers and you jump from bed. But it hurt to hear him laugh, almost as much as to see him sad. Cruel, sweet hurt. She didn't

know why. And to love him was like you owned a labor
of land, and could walk on out and breathe the air of it,
and eat the food it grew you; no, it was like *she* was the
land, and she would feed him, and he would breathe
her; no, or both.

O Bernardino, cover me with the shadow of your
hand.

Bernardino had fetched the turkey. He set it on the
ground in front of Jensie, its legs stiff as stone, its
feathers soft against the stones. It was a big bird.

Bernardino looked at her.

Jensie smiled. She said, "Yes, I am very hungry."

"*Huchaa!*" Bernardino shouted. He was happy. Jensie
laughed to see him.

They plucked the bird. Its feathers popped from its
pebbled skin, sometimes in whole handfuls, sometimes
one tight quill by one tight quill. Next thing they knew,
they were blowing feathers at each other and both
laughing like crazy. They rolled in the feathers and
puffed feathers at each other's faces and scattered
feathers everywhere. Feathers floating in the air. Their
laughter floating in the air. That turkey's show was
scattered everywhere, across the ground, among the
rocks, up in the walnut tree and in Jensie's hair. In
Bernardino's hair. Down their backs even.

Feathers among their kisses even. But that gobbler
turkey was watching. He was so glum. So they cooked
him. They gutted him and put him on a stick. Bernardino got a fire started from the pan of his rifle. Then he
and Jensie broke dead branches from the walnut clump,
and fetched a chunk of dead mesquite from the canyon
side, and built a first-rate fire. When the fire was down
to coals and the mesquite smoke pale they put that

turkey above it and had him do a dance. Pretty soon his fat was squeaking through the pinholes and steaming and sputting onto the coals. It was nigh more than Jensie and Bernardino could stand. They had to stand it, though. They had to cook that old acorn-eater a long while, he was such a big one. He was a juicy one. He was a tasty-smelling one. He was a crisp-skinned, shrunk-loose-from-the-hocks, breast-busted, sweet-smoke-smelling, speckle-burnt, deep-turkey-meated, juicy one, and it was more than a body could hardly stand. Finally they couldn't stand it any longer. They lit into him.

He was hot. He burnt their fingers. He made their fingers greasy. They pulled off his drumsticks. His skin was so crisp it crackle-split. And the cooked joints undid. Then he lay open, all dark-turkey-meat and steaming. They chunked the meat into their mouths. It was good. It was hot and turkey in their mouths. But all at once Jensie was thinking about how, when they come to her folks' place, there would be *more* good things to eat. Now whatever was the matter with her? It seemed like she was hungry even when she was eating! Jensie giggled. Bernardino glanced across at her. He looked so funny with his mouth full of turkey, and Jensie giggled some more. And when they come to her folks' place, there'd be things to eat that Jensie bet Bernardino hadn't ever eaten before. She bet he hadn't ever eaten poor-doo, or cush with a lot of onions in it, or pumpkin bread, or okra. Her mama could cook all those things. Jensie could too, because her mama had showed her. And pretty soon it would be the time of year for a green-grape pie.

Jensie said, "Bernardino, when we get home, Mama

and I will cook you a green-grape pie. Then you can eat it."

Bernardino said, "I would like that, Grullita."

Well, here was the wishbone, but the bullet had broken it. So they couldn't make a wish.

The breast meat come loose easy from the keel. It was dry and stringy and white, even if it was wild. It pulled apart easy. But Jensie'd had her fill. "¡Ay!" she said. She lay back against a rock. That felt good. The fire near her feet felt good. The turkey in her belly felt awful good. There was a greasy good taste around her mouth. And her daddy could teach Bernardino things. To mend harness and split shingles and to rive with a froe. Her daddy knew how to make a tumbler by burning a string around a bottle and then filing the edges smooth with a stone, and he could teach Bernardino.

Jensie said, "Bernardino, when we get home my father will teach you a hundred things. To read, even. Mi padre can read. And we'll go down and help him work in the bottoms."

Bernardino didn't say anything for a while. Then he said, softly, "I would like to do that."

And this here river, it was open to the morning sun, clear and trickle-tongued, didn't need to keep no secrets. That gravel bar over there was busted out now into a sight of purple phlox. This river had rolled those washed-up stones from far lonesome places, yes, but now look at it. Rich and flowersome and free.

This here river.

It owned itself. It owned this whole valley. It bent the tallest sun to cool onto its dapple rocks.

This here river.

Oh this here river!

And here, in this sudden meadow place, it was freest, openest of all. The grass upward grew. The trees upward and upward grew. That was all this here river ever had to know, and it knew it for ever and ever.

A man was standing in the lower end of the meadow. He had stepped out of the hackberries. He was eyeing Bernardino and Jensie.

Jensie reined in her coyote. Bernardino trotted up alongside her. "Siga—keep going," he said.

They rode together down across the meadow.

The man was leaning on his rifle, one knee bent. He had his head tilted back, eyeing them. It wasn't until Jensie was up close that she could see it was because his left eyelid drooped that he had to tilt his head back that way, in order to see out of it.

The man squinted up at them from the slant of his head. He waited until they were up close. Then his right eye blinked. But not the other eye.

Bernardino and Jensie looked down at him. He stood stock still, looking right back. His face was corncob red. It was splotched with rusty freckles. His eyebrows were a rusty red and long as switches, and his eyelashes were orange, stiff as the lashes of a hog's eyes. Red. Red thicket in each ear. His hair red, red as fire almost. And his beard a brighter red still, and full-up of whatever he'd spat across it. He spat across it right now. He squinted his blue eye up at Jensie from the tilt of his head.

"Halloo," Jensie said.

The man squinted up at her. It wrinkled the scar that cut across his cheek, half hid by beard. He reminded

Jensie of an old, cracked, yellow gourd, left too long in the bucket and gone to mold. Especially his beard and his leather, sweaty-black clothes reminded her of it.

His beard twitched. He said, "I'd a-never a-reckoned hit."

"What does he say?" Bernardino said. He was looking at that scar.

"Yo no sé," Jensie said.

"¿Quién es él?" Bernardino said.

"Yo no sé quién es."

"Talk Meskin like a regular greaser, don' ye," the man drawled. "But I know thet white hair."

Jensie looked at him. The man squinted harder than ever. Jensie said, "¿Señor, conoce usted . . .?"

"I don't talk hit," the Texan drawled. He spat across his beard.

"Do you know my daddy?"

The Texan grinned, all yellow-toothed among red beard.

"I reckon. Holped him to put in his spring plantin'."

"¡Ay, Bernardino!" Jensie said. "¡Él conoce a mi padre!"

The Texan squinted at her. "If hit don't beat all," he said.

Jensie slid from the coyote. "Is my mama all right? Is my daddy all right?" she said.

"I reckon."

"Is little Dee all right?"

"Sometimes he gits to cryin' after ye."

"¡Ay!" Jensie said. It was might'near more than she could stand. She pushed her head into the coyote's neck. The critter breathed and shifted.

Bernardino said, "What does he say, Grullita?"

¡Ay! Mi madre, sus manos arrugadas de tanto lavar. Mi padre, trabaja todo el día en el campo por amor de nosotros. Y mi hermano, a quien fui tan mala, llora por mí. Ellos se acuerdan de mí: My mama's hands all wrinkled from washing. My daddy working all day in the bottoms, to spell out his love for us. And little Dee, that I was mean to, crying after me. They remember me.

Now she seen their faces.

"They remember me!" she said.

Bernardino said, "Do not cry, Jensi."

"I want to go home, Bernardino," Jensie said.

Bernardino looked at her. Then he looked down at the mule's neck.

"We will go home now, Bernardino," Jensie said.

Bernardino's fingers twisted and untwisted in the mule's mane. He talked down at the mule's neck. He looked at the Texan. Bernardino said, "¿Jensi?"

"¿Sí?" Jensie said.

"This man knows your father?"

"Sí, Bernardino," Jensie said.

"He is a friend to your father?"

"He says he has worked with him."

"He is a tejano?"

"Sí."

Bernardino stared at the mule's neck. He said, "Then go with him. He will take you to your home."

"What do you mean?"

Bernardino said, "I cannot go with you."

"¿Qué estás diciendo, Bernardino?" Jensie said.

Bernardino unsnagged his fingers from the tangled mane. "Yo voy a Méjico," he said.

Jensie ran to him. His face was turned away. She

grabbed his knee. The mule shied away. Its gear rattled and the crosstree creaked.

"Do not touch me," Bernardino whispered. "He is watching us."

"You said you would go home with me!"

Bernardino said, "Yo voy a Méjico."

"I love you!" Jensie said.

The mule shied sideways from Jensie. Bernardino held him. He whispered, "¡Por favor! ¡Por favor! *Please. Please.* He is watching us."

Jensie said, "*You said you would go home with me!*"

Bernardino laid the reins against the mule's neck. The mule pivoted. Bernardino held him.

"Ya está," Bernardino said.

"¿Qué? ¿Qué?"

"I am a Mexican."

"¡Ay! ¡Ay!" Jensie all at once cried. "*¿Entonces has mentido?*" Rage looped through her like a dry-as-dust rope. "*¿Entonces tú me has mentido?—then did you lie to me? Was it all a lie?*"

Bernardino said, "I cannot go home with you."

Jensie stared, her fists squeezing her dress, crumpling it.

"¡Bandido!" she suddenly screamed.

"¡Ay, Jensi!"

"¡Bandido! ¡Bandido! ¡Bandido!" Jensie screamed. It come out like knots of rope jerking from her gullet.

Bernardino looked at her. Jensie said, "You are like Toral! You are like el Nahuatl!"

Bernardino blinked. He said, "Adiós." He gave the mule a kick and started to ride up the meadow. The coyote whinnied. The mule honked back. Then the blue coyote took off after them, trotting, its gourds bobbing, its head pumping, its reins dragging in the grass.

"¡Bandido! ¡Bandido!" Jensie hollered. Her rage lifted her up onto her toes—it was like a bone had cracked when the rifle cracked behind her.

Bernardino's arms flung up. He fell sideways to the ground.

"¡Qué has hecho!"

Smoke curled from the Texan's rifle. "No use to waste them horses," he said.

"¡Diablo!" Jensie screamed. She ran to Bernardino. She ran as hard as she could. It took all her breath.

When she got to him, he was lying on his back. "Bernardino!" Jensie said.

He looked up at Jensie. He didn't seem too bad hurt. He tried to smile. "Grullita," he said.

He said, "I could not have lived without you."

But that man was walking up.

Jensie jumped to her feet. The mule was near by. Jensie grabbed the mosquete. She spun around and aimed it.

"¡Vete!" she yelled. "¡Vete! ¡Vete!"

The Texan stopped in his tracks. He squinted at her from the slant of his head.

"Gone plumb wild," he said.

He took another step toward her.

"¡Yo te voy a matar!" Jensie said. *I'll kill you!* She pointed the musket at him.

The Texan squinted his eyes at her. His beard shone fiery red in the sun. He spat across it. He wiped the back of his wrist across it. He didn't say anything for a minute. Then he said, "No, you wouldn't do that." He said, "I'm yore own kind."

"*¡Yo te voy a matar!*" Jensie said.

"Jist been a-livin' too long with 'em is all. Yew'll git over hit."

He squinted at her. He said, "Wal, I'll go fetch yore paw." He turned and started down the meadow.

Jensie swayed from side to side. It was like the whole world was spinning, about to pitch her at him, to bite into his neck, *oh to fix him good* with a bullet smack between his shoulder blades, splat his red hair redder yet, nor wonder at all if his blood come black, or if his heart come out tumbling black. And now she had him in her sights. But never pulled the trigger. Now he was gone into the hackberries and it was too late.

Jensie sank to the ground. The mosquete clattered to the ground. Jensie ran her fingers through her hair, pulled hard at her hair. She took a deep breath.

She looked at Bernardino. She said, "Well, now you've *got* to come home."

She crawled on her hands and knees to him. His hand was stretched out to her. He was still smiling.

But his eyes were so wide, looking up.

She said, "Bernardino?"

She touched his hand. It gave way to hers.

She said, "Bernardino!"

She touched his face. It turned to her. His eyes! They seemed so solid in their stare.

Bernardino!

She scrambled up to him. She pulled open his serape. He's not hurt! Thank God, he's not hurt.

His head turned like a toy.

"*Bernardino!*"

And held him to her. And when she lifted him up, she seen his whole story; the ground was soaked with it.

But look! His lips! Moved! His wrist: about to lift, about to wipe that milky stare from his eyes—*see it stir? See that hump of a pulse through it?*

The shadow of a bird.

No he ain't dead.

O say something!

Bernardino.

¡Mi Bernardino!

And held him, and rocked him back and forth, back and forth in her arms, the wet grass squeaking underneath.

These are your lips. These are the bruises in your face I kiss. These are the dear warm cheeks, here, where I kiss. You were . . . so gentle . . . back of them. This is your black hair I brush back from your face. O my dear one, my dear one! This is your face. O how can I ever tell you with my breath? How can I kiss your eyes enough to know? My heart, my love, my child, my child! I kiss your wrists; o these, these are your dear, dear hands I kiss. They are so. Slender. O my dear love. My dear love. How can I ever kiss your hands enough to know?

He is so quiet from me.

Jensie shook all over. A cruel pain stabbed through her, into her belly, into her lowest places, and cut, and twisted, and let up a thin animal cry from out of her.

Then come her breath. Then come her creaking sobs.

She fetched him to the river. She laid him out careful on the grass and washed him and covered him. She watched with him. Up in the broomwillows a brown wife fretted *check check check* from her nest; from down the river somewhere her mate cried *o-ka-leee*— then he come flashing back, beating his red-patch wings, fetching things. And this here river . . .

Never see you more?

O goodbye. Goodbye. Goodbye. Do you know what that means? Do you know what that means? Adiós. *Adiós.* O goodbye, goodbye, goodbye!

I am nothing. Nada.

I will be always with you.

And night come on. And a night breeze come down from the plateau. And it seemed like in the settling dark his skin was getting lighter and lighter, until only it was his bruises that were dark.

And night come on.

Then she heard her daddy calling Jensie.